Beautiful
Joe

The
GOLDEN PRESS
Classics Library

Beautiful
JOE

by Marshall Saunders

MODERN ABRIDGED EDITION

Illustrated by Robert MacLean

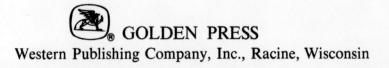

GOLDEN PRESS

Western Publishing Company, Inc., Racine, Wisconsin

Library of Congress Catalog Card Number 65-11914

CONTENTS

Beautiful
Joe

I

Only a Cur

MY NAME is Beautiful Joe, and I am a brown dog of medium size. I am not beautiful, and I am not a thorough-bred. I am only a cur.

I was born in a stable on the outskirts of a small town in Maine called Fairport. The first thing I remember is lying close to my mother and being very snug and warm. The next thing I remember is being always hungry. I had a number of brothers and sisters—six in all—and my mother never had enough milk for us. She was always half starved herself, so she could not feed us properly.

I am very unwilling to say much about my early life. I have lived so long in a family where there is never a harsh word spoken, and where no one thinks of ill-treating anybody or anything, that it seems almost wrong to think or speak of such a matter as hurting a poor dumb beast.

The man that owned my mother was a milkman. He kept one horse and three cows, and he had a shaky old cart that he used to put his milk cans in. It makes me shudder now to think of him. His name was Jenkins, and I am glad he is being punished now for his cruelty to poor dumb animals and to human beings. If you think it is wrong for me to be glad, you must remember that I am only a dog.

The first notice that he took of me when I was a little puppy, just able to stagger about, was to give me a kick that sent me into a corner of the stable. He used to beat and starve my mother. I have seen him use a heavy whip to punish her. When I got older I asked her why she did not run away. She said she did not wish to; but I soon found out that she did not run away because she loved Jenkins. Cruel and savage as he was, she loved him, and I believe she would have laid down her life for her master if need be.

Now that I am old, I know that there are many men in the world like Jenkins; men who seem to be possessed with a spirit of wickedness. One reason for Jenkins's cruelty was his idleness. After he went his rounds in the morning with his milk cans, he had nothing to do till late in the afternoon but take care of his stable and yard. If he had kept them neat, and groomed his horse, and cleaned his cows, and dug up the garden, it would have taken up all his time. But he never tidied the place at all, till his yard and stable got so littered up with things he threw down that he could not make his way about.

I used to wish that some of the people that took milk from him would come and look at his cows. In the spring and summer he drove them out to pasture, but during the winter they stood all the time in the dirty, dark stable, where the chinks in the wall were so big that the snow swept through in drifts. The ground was always muddy and wet. There was only one small window on the north side, where the sun shone in for only a very short time in the afternoon.

They were very unhappy cows, but they stood patiently and never complained, though sometimes I know they must have nearly frozen in the bitter winds that blew through the stable on winter nights. They were lean and poor, and were never in good health. Besides being cold they were fed on very poor food.

Jenkins used to come home nearly every afternoon with a great tub in the back of his cart that was full of what he called "peelings." It was kitchen stuff that he asked the cooks to save for him at the different houses where he delivered milk. They threw spoiled vegetables, fruit parings, and scraps from the table into a tub, and gave them to him at the end of a few days. This food, together with poor hay, was all he fed the cows. Consequently they gave very poor milk, and Jenkins used to put white powder in it, to give it "body," he said.

Once a very sad thing happened about the milk, that no one knew about but Jenkins and his wife. She was a poor, unhappy creature, very frightened of her husband, and not daring to speak much to him. She was not a clean woman, and I never saw a worse-looking house than the one she kept.

The children used to play in mud puddles about the door. It was the youngest of them that sickened with some kind of fever early in the spring, before Jenkins began driving the cows out to pasture. The child was very ill, and Mrs. Jenkins wanted to send for a doctor, but her husband would not let her. They made a bed in the kitchen, close to the stove, and Mrs. Jenkins nursed the child as best she could. She did all her work nearby, and I saw her several times wiping the child's face with the cloth that she used for washing her milk pans.

Nobody knew outside the family that the little girl was ill. Jenkins had such a bad name that none of the neighbors would visit them. By-and-by the child got well. But a week or two later Jenkins came home with quite a frightened face, and told his wife that the husband of one of his customers was very ill with typhoid fever.

After a time the gentleman died, and the cook told Jenkins that the doctor wondered how he could have taken the fever, for there was not a case in town.

There was a widow left with three orphans, and they never knew that a careless milkman was to blame for taking a kind husband and father from them.

2

The Cruel Milkman

I HAVE said that Jenkins spent most of his days in idleness. He had to start out very early in the morning, in order to supply his customers with milk for breakfast. Oh, how ugly he used to be, when he came into the stable on cold winter mornings, before the sun was up.

He would hang his lantern on a hook, and get his milking stool, and if the cows did not step aside just to suit him, he would seize a broom or fork and beat them cruelly.

My mother and I slept on a heap of straw in the corner of the stable, and when she heard his step in the morning she always roused me, so that we could run outdoors as soon as he opened the stable door. He always aimed a kick at us as we passed, but my mother taught me how to dodge him.

After he finished milking, he took the pails of milk up to the house for Mrs. Jenkins to strain and put in the cans, and he came back and harnessed his horse to the cart. His horse was called Toby, and a poor, miserable, broken-down creature he was. He was weak in the knees, and weak in the back, and weak all over, and Jenkins beat him all the time to make him go. He had been a cab horse, and his mouth had been jerked and twisted and sawed at till one would think there could be no feeling left in it. Still I have seen him wince and curl his lip when Jenkins thrust in the frosty bit on a winter morning.

After Jenkins put him in the cart, and took in the cans, he set out on his rounds. My mother, whose name was Jess, always went with him. I used to ask her why she followed such a brute of a man, and she would hang her head and say that sometimes she got a bone from the different houses where they stopped. But that was not the whole reason. She liked Jenkins so much that she wanted to be with him.

I had not her sweet and patient disposition, and I would not go with her. I watched her out of sight, and then ran up to the house to see if Mrs. Jenkins had any scraps for me. I nearly always got something, for she pitied me and often gave me a kind word or look with the bits of food that she threw to me.

When Jenkins came home, I often coaxed Mother to run about and see some of the neighbors' dogs with me. But she never would, and I would not leave her. So from morning to night we had to sneak about, keeping out of Jenkins's way as much as we could, and yet trying to keep him in sight. He always sauntered about with a pipe in his mouth and his hands in his pockets, growling first at his wife and children, and then at his dumb creatures.

I have not told what became of my brothers and sisters. One rainy day when we were eight weeks old, Jenkins, followed by two or three of his ragged, dirty children, came into the stable and looked at us. Then he began to swear because we were so ugly, and said if we had been good-looking he might have sold some of us. Mother watched him anxiously, and, fearing some danger to her puppies, she ran and jumped in the middle of us and looked pleadingly up at him.

It only made him swear the more. He took one pup after another, and right there put an end to their lives. I don't know why he spared me. I was the only one left.

His children cried, and he sent them out of the stable and went out himself. Mother picked up all the puppies, brought them to our nest in the straw and licked them, and tried to bring them back to life. But it was no use; they were quite dead.

My mother never seemed the same after this. She was weak and miserable, and though she was only four years old, she seemed like an old dog. One day she licked me gently, wagged her tail, and died.

As I sat by her, feeling lonely and miserable, Jenkins came into the stable. I could not bear to look at him. He had killed my mother. Oh, how I hated him! But I sat quietly, even when he went and turned her over with his foot to see if she was really dead. I think he was a little sorry, for he turned scornfully toward me and said, "She was worth two of you. Why didn't you go instead?"

Still I kept quiet till he walked up to me and kicked at me. My heart was nearly broken, and I could stand no more. I flew at him in a rage and gave him a savage bite on the ankle.

"Oho!" he said. "So you are going to be a fighter, are you?

I'll fix you for that." His face was red and furious. He seized me by the back of the neck and carried me out to the yard where a log lay on the ground. "Bill!" he called to one of his children. "Bring me the hatchet."

He laid my head on the log and pressed one hand on my struggling body. I was now a year old and a full-sized dog. There was a quick, dreadful pain, and he had cut off my ear, not in the way they cut puppies' ears, but close to my head, so close that he cut off some of the skin beyond it. Then he cut off the other ear and, turning me swiftly round, he cut off my tail close to my body.

Then he let me go and stood looking at me as I rolled on the ground and yelped in agony. He was in such a passion that he did not think that people passing by on the road might hear me.

3

My Kind Deliverer
and Miss Laura

THERE WAS a young man going by on a bicycle. He heard my screams and, springing off his bicycle, he came hurrying up the path. He stood among us before Jenkins caught sight of him.

In the midst of my pain, I heard him say fiercely, "What have you been doing to that dog?"

"I've been cuttin' his ears for fightin', my young gentleman," said Jenkins. "There's no law to prevent that."

"And there is no law to prevent my giving you a beating," said the young man angrily. In a trice he had seized Jenkins by the throat and was pounding him with all his might. Mrs. Jenkins came and stood at the house door crying, but making no effort to help her husband.

"Bring me a towel," the young man cried to her, after he had stretched Jenkins, bruised and frightened, on the ground. She snatched off her apron and ran down with it. The young man wrapped me in it and, taking me carefully in his arms, walked down the path to the gate. There were some little boys standing there watching him, their mouths wide open with astonishment.

"Sonny," he said to the largest one of the boys, "if you will come along behind and carry this dog, I will give you a quarter."

The boy took me, and we set out. I was all smothered up in the apron and moaning with pain, but still I looked out occasionally to see which way we were going. We took the road to the town and stopped in front of a house on Washington Street. The young man leaned his bicycle up against the house, took a quarter from his pocket, and put it in the boy's hand. Then, lifting me gently in his arms, he went up a lane leading to the back of the house.

There was a small stable there. He went into it, put me down on the floor, and uncovered my body. Some boys were playing about the stable and I heard them say in horrified tones, "Oh, Cousin Harry! What is the matter with that dog?"

"Hush," he said. "Don't make a fuss. You, Jack, go down to the kitchen and ask Mary for a basin of warm water and a sponge, and don't let your mother or Laura hear you."

A few minutes later, the young man had bathed my bleeding ears and tail, and had rubbed something on them that was cool and pleasant, and had bandaged them firmly with strips of cotton. I felt much better and was able to look about me.

I was in a small stable, that was evidently not used for a stable, but more for a playroom. There were various kinds of

toys scattered about, and a swing and a bar, such as boys love to twist about on, in two different corners. In a box against the wall was a guinea pig, looking at me in an interested way. This guinea pig's name was Jeff, and he and I became good friends. A long-haired French rabbit was hopping about, and a tame white rat was perched on the shoulder of one of the boys and kept his foothold there, no matter how suddenly the boy moved. There were so many boys, and the stable was so small, that I suppose he was afraid he would get stepped on if he went on the floor. He stared hard at me with his little red eyes, and never even glanced at a queer-looking gray cat that was watching me, too, from her bed in the back of the vacant horse stall. Out in the sunny yard, some pigeons were pecking grain, and a spaniel lay asleep in a corner.

I had never seen anything like this before, and my wonder at it almost drove the pain away. Mother and I always chased rats and birds, and once we killed a kitten. While I was puzzling over it, one of the boys cried out, "Here is Laura!"

"Take that rag out of the way," said Mr. Harry, kicking aside the old apron I had been wrapped in. One of the boys stuffed it into a barrel, and then they all looked toward the house.

A young girl, holding up one hand to shade her eyes from the sun, was coming up the walk that led from the house to the stable. I thought that I had never seen such a beautiful girl, and I think so still. She was tall and slender, and had lovely brown eyes and brown hair, and a sweet smile. Just to look at her was enough to make one love her. I stood in the stable door, staring at her with all my might.

"Why, what a funny dog," she said, and stopped short to look at me. Up to this, I had not thought what a queer-looking

sight I must be. Now I twisted round my head, saw the white
bandage on my tail, and, knowing I was not a fit spectacle for
a pretty young lady like that, I slunk into a corner.

"Poor doggie, have I hurt your feelings?" she said, and
with a sweet smile at the boys she passed by them and came
up to the guinea pig's box, behind which I had gone.

"What is the matter with your head, good dog?" she said
curiously, as she stooped over me.

"Dear Laura." The young man came up and laid his hand
on her shoulder. "He got hurt, and I have been bandaging
him."

"Who hurt him?"

"I had rather not tell you."

"But I wish to know." Her voice was as gentle as ever, but
she spoke so decidedly that the young man was obliged to tell
her everything. All the time he was speaking, she kept touching me gently with her fingers. When he had finished his account of rescuing me from Jenkins, she said quietly, "You
will have the man punished?"

"What is the use? Punishing him won't stop him from
being cruel."

"It will put a check on his cruelty."

"I don't think it would do any good," said the young man
doggedly.

"Cousin Harry!" The young girl stood up very straight and
tall, her brown eyes flashing, and one hand pointed at me.
"Will you let that pass? That animal has been wronged, and
it looks to you to right the wrong. The coward who has
maimed it for life should be punished. A child has a voice to
tell its wrong—a poor, dumb creature must suffer in silence;
in bitter, bitter silence." She went on quickly as the young

man tried to interrupt her. "And you are doing the man himself an injustice. If he is bad enough to ill-treat his dog, he will ill-treat his wife and children. If he is checked and punished now for his cruelty, he may reform. And even if his wicked heart is not changed, he will be obliged to treat them with outward kindness, through fear of punishment."

The young man looked convinced, and almost as ashamed as if he had been the one to crop my ears.

"What do you want me to do?" he said. "I'm only a visitor here, you know."

The girl pulled a little watch from her belt. "I want you to report that man immediately. It is now five o'clock. I will go down to the police station with you, if you like."

"Very well," he said, his face brightening, and together they went off to the house.

4

The Morris Boys Add
to My Name

The boys watched them out of sight. Then the one called Jack gave a low whistle and said, "Doesn't Laura come out strong when anyone or anything gets abused?"

They all came and bent over me, as I lay on the floor in my corner. I wasn't much used to boys, and I didn't know how they would treat me. But I soon found by the way they handled me and talked to me, that they knew a good deal about dogs and were accustomed to treating them kindly. It seemed very strange to have the boys pat me and call me "good dog." No one had ever said such a thing to me before today.

"He's certainly not much of a beauty, is he?" said one of the boys.

"Not by a long shot," said Jack Morris with a laugh. "Not

any nearer the beauty mark than you are, Tom."

Tom flew at him, and they had a scuffle. The other boys paid no attention to them but went on looking at me. One of them, a little boy with eyes like Miss Laura's, said, "What did Cousin Harry say the dog's name was?"

"Joe," answered another boy. "The little chap that carried him home told him."

"We might call him 'Ugly Joe' then," said a lad with a round fat face and laughing eyes. I found out later that he was another of Miss Laura's brothers, and his name was Ned. There seemed to be no end to the Morris boys.

"I don't think Laura would like that," said Jack Morris, suddenly coming up behind him. He was very hot and was breathing fast, but his manner was as cool as if he had never left the group about me. He had beaten Tom, who was sitting on a box, ruefully surveying a hole in his jacket. "You see," Jack went on, "if you call him 'Ugly,' her ladyship will say that you are wounding the dear dog's feelings. 'Beautiful Joe' would be more to her liking."

A shout went up from the boys. I didn't wonder that they laughed. Plain-looking I naturally was, but I must have been hideous in those bandages.

" 'Beautiful Joe' then let it be!" they cried. "Let's go and tell Mother, and ask her to give us something for our beauty to eat."

They all trooped out of the stable, and I was very sorry, for when they were with me I did not mind so much the tingling in my ears and the terrible pain in my back. They soon brought me some nice food, but I could not touch it. They went away to their play, and I lay in the box, trembling with pain.

By and by it got dark. I saw lights twinkling in the windows of the house. I felt lonely and miserable in this strange place. I would not have gone back to Jenkins for the world. But that was the only home I had known, and though I felt that I should be happy here, I had not yet got used to the change. And the pain all through my body was dreadful. My head seemed to be on fire, and there were sharp, darting pains up and down my backbone.

At last I could bear the pain no longer. I sat up in my box and looked around me. I slunk into the yard and along the stable wall, where there was a thick clump of raspberry bushes. I crept in among them and lay down in the damp earth. I tried to scratch off my bandages, but they were fastened on too firmly, and I could not do it. I thought about my poor mother and wished she were here to lick my sore ears and soothe my pain.

In the midst of my trouble I heard a soft voice calling, "Joe! Joe!" It was Miss Laura's voice, but I felt as if there were weights on my paws, and I could not go to her.

"Joe! Joe!" she said again. She was going up the walk to the stable, holding a lighted lamp in her hand. I watched her disappear into the stable. She did not stay there long. She came out and stood on the gravel. Then she saw me and came to the spot where I was.

"Poor doggie," she said, stooping down and patting me. "Are you very miserable?" She set her lamp on the ground and took me in her arms. "But of course you are."

I was very thin then, but still I was quite an armful for her. But she did not seem to find me heavy. She took me right into the house, through the back door and down a long flight of steps, across a hall, and into a snug kitchen.

"For the land sakes, Miss Laura," said a woman who was

bending over a stove. "What have you got there?"

"A poor sick dog, Mary," said Laura, seating herself on a chair. "Will you please warm a little milk for him? And have you a box or a basket down here that he can lie in?"

"I guess so," said the woman. "But he's awful dirty. You're not going to let him sleep in the house, are you?"

"Only for tonight. He is very ill. A dreadful thing happened to him, Mary." And Miss Laura went on to tell her how my ears had been cut off.

"Oh, that's the dog the boys were talking about," said the woman. "Poor creature, he's welcome to all I can do for him." She brought out a box and folded a piece of blanket for me to lie on. Then she heated some milk in a saucepan, poured it in a saucer, and watched me while Miss Laura went upstairs to get a little bottle of something that would make me sleep. They poured a few drops of this medicine into the milk and offered it to me. After the milk was gone, Mary lifted up my box and carried me into the washroom that was off the kitchen.

I soon fell sound asleep, and could not rouse myself through the night, even though I both smelled and heard someone coming near me several times. The next morning I found out that it was Miss Laura.

5

My New Home
and a Selfish Lady

In a week, thanks to good nursing, good food, and kind words, I was almost well. Mr. Harry washed and dressed my sore ears and tail every day till he went home, and one day he and the boys gave me a bath out in the stable. They carried out a tub of warm water and stood me in it. I had never been washed before in my life, and it felt very queer, and also very nice.

Two days after I arrived at the Morrises', Jack and the other boys came running into the stable. Jack had a newspaper in his hand and, with a great deal of laughing and joking, he read this to me:

" 'FAIRPORT DAILY NEWS, June third. In the police court this morning James Jenkins was fined ten dollars and costs for cruelly torturing and mutilating a dog.' "

Jack threw the paper into my box, and he and the other boys gave three cheers for the DAILY NEWS and then ran away. How glad I was! It did not matter so much for me, for I had escaped him, but now that it had been found out what a cruel man he was, there would be a restraint upon him, and poor Toby and the cows would have a happier time.

I was going to tell about the Morris family. There were Mr. Morris, who was a clergyman and preached in a church in Fairport; Mrs. Morris, his wife; Miss Laura, who was the eldest of the family; then Jack, Ned, Carl, and Willie.

Mr. Morris was a very busy man and rarely interfered in household affairs. Mrs. Morris was the one who said what was to be done and what was not to be done. There was never any noise or confusion in the house, and though there was a great deal of work to be done, everything went on smoothly and pleasantly. Mrs. Morris was a very wise and good woman. She had definite ideas on how children should be reared.

Mrs. Morris was very particular about money matters. Whenever the boys came to her for money for selfish things, she said firmly: "No, my children. We are not rich people, and we must save our money for your education. I cannot give you money with which to buy foolish things."

But if they asked her for money for books or something to make their pet animals more comfortable, or for their outdoor games which they shared together, she gave it to them willingly.

One fine June day Mrs. Morris was sewing in a rocking chair by the window. I was beside her, sitting on a hassock, so that I could look out into the street. Dogs love variety and excitement, and like to see what is going on outdoors as well as human beings. A carriage drove up to the door, and a finely dressed lady got out and came up the steps.

Mrs. Morris seemed glad to see her and called her Mrs. Montague. I was pleased with her, for she had some kind of perfume about her that I liked to smell. So I went and sat on the hearth rug quite near her.

They had a little talk about things I did not understand, and then the lady's eyes fell on me. She looked at me through a bit of glass that was hanging by a chain from her neck, and pulled away her beautiful dress lest I should touch it.

I did not care any longer for the perfume and went away and sat very straight and stiff at Mrs. Morris's feet. The lady's eyes still followed me.

"I beg your pardon, Mrs. Morris," she said, "but that is a very queer-looking dog you have there."

"Yes," said Mrs. Morris quietly. "He is not a very handsome dog."

"He is a new one, isn't he?" said Mrs. Montague.

"Yes."

"And that makes—"

"Two dogs, a cat, fifteen or twenty rabbits, a rat, about a dozen canaries, two dozen goldfish, I don't know how many pigeons, a few bantams, a guinea pig, and—well, I don't think there is anything more."

They both laughed, and Mrs. Montague said, "You have quite a menagerie. My father would never allow one of his children to keep a pet animal. He said it would make his girls rough and noisy to romp about the house with cats, and his boys would look like rowdies if they went about with dogs at their heels."

"I have never found that it made my children rough to play

with their pets," said Mrs. Morris.

"No, I should think not," said the lady languidly. "Your boys are the most gentlemanly lads in Fairport, and as for Laura, she is a perfect little lady. I like so much to have them come and see Charlie. They wake him up and yet don't make him naughty."

"They enjoyed their last visit very much," said Mrs. Morris. "By the way, I have heard them talking about getting Charlie a dog."

"Oh!" cried the lady, with a little shudder. "Beg them not to! I cannot sanction that. I hate dogs!"

"Why do you hate them?" asked Mrs. Morris gently.

"They are such dirty things. They always smell and have vermin on them."

"A dog," said Mrs. Morris, "is something like a child. If you want it clean and pleasant, you have to keep it so. This dog's skin is as clean as yours or mine. Hold still, Joe." And she brushed the hair on my back the wrong way, and showed Mrs. Montague how pink and free from dust my skin was.

Mrs. Montague looked at me more kindly, and even held out the tips of her fingers to me. I did not lick them. I only smelled them, and she drew her hand back again.

"You have never been brought in contact with the lower creatures as I have," said Mrs. Morris. "Just let me tell you what a help dumb animals have been to me in the upbringing of my children—my boys, especially. Laura is naturally unselfish. I have never had any trouble with her. But the boys, though good boys in most ways, as they grew older thought of nothing but themselves. It was each one for himself, and they used to quarrel with each other in regard to their rights.

"While we were in New York, we had only a small back yard. When we came here, I decided to try an experiment. We got this house because it had a large garden and a stable that would do for the boys to play in. Then I called them together and had a serious little talk.

"I said I was not pleased with the way in which they were living. They did nothing for anyone but themselves from morning to night. If I asked them to do an errand for me, it was done unwillingly. Of course, I knew they had their school for a part of the day, but they had a good deal of leisure time when they might do something for someone else. I asked them if they thought they were going to make real, manly Christian boys at this rate, and they said no. Then I asked them what we should do about it. They all said, 'Tell us, Mother, and we'll do as you say.'

"I proposed a series of tasks. If I could have afforded it, I would have got a horse and cow, and had the boys take charge of them. But I could not do that; so I invested in a pair of rabbits for Jack, a pair of canaries for Carl, pigeons for Ned, and bantams for Willie. I brought these creatures home, put them into the boys' hands, and told them to provide for them. The boys were delighted with my choice, and it was very amusing to see them scurrying to provide food and shelter for their pets, and to hear their consultations with other boys.

"The end of it all is that I am perfectly satisfied with my experiment. My boys, in caring for these dumb creatures, have become unselfish and thoughtful. It keeps them at home. I don't mean to say we have deprived them of liberty. They have their days for baseball and football and excursions to the woods, but they have so much to do at home that they don't go anywhere else except for a specific purpose."

While Mrs. Morris was talking, her visitor leaned forward in her chair and listened attentively. When she finished, Mrs. Montague said quietly, "Thank you. I am glad you told me this. I shall get Charlie a dog."

"I am glad to hear you say that," replied Mrs. Morris. "It will be a good thing for your little boy. I should not wish my boys to be without a good, faithful dog. A child can learn many a lesson from a dog. This one," pointing to me, "might be held up as an example to many a human being. He is patient, quiet, and obedient. My husband says that he reminds him of three words in the Bible—'through much tribulation.' "

"Why does he say that?" asked Mrs. Montague in a curious tone.

"Because he came to us from a very unhappy home." And Mrs. Morris went on to tell her friend what she knew of my early days.

When she stopped, Mrs. Montague's face was shocked and pained. "How dreadful to think that there are such creatures as that man Jenkins in the world. And you say that he has a wife and children. Mrs. Morris, tell me plainly, are there many such unhappy homes in Fairport?"

Mrs. Morris hesitated for a minute. Then she said earnestly, "My dear friend, if you could see all the wickedness and cruelty and vileness that are practiced in this little town of ours in one night, you could not rest in your bed."

Mrs. Montague looked dazed. "I did not dream that it was as bad as that," she said. "Are we worse than the people in other towns?"

"No, not worse, but bad enough. Over and over again the saying is true, one-half the world does not know how the other half lives. How can all this misery touch you? You live in your lovely house out of the town. When you come in, you drive about, do your shopping, make calls, and go home again. You never visit the poorer streets. The people from them never come to you. You are rich, your people before you were rich, and you live practically in a state of isolation."

"But that is not right," said the lady in a wailing voice. "I have been thinking about this matter lately. I read a great deal in the papers about the misery of the lower classes, and I think we richer ones ought to do something to help them. Mrs. Morris, what can I do?"

Tears came into Mrs. Morris's eyes. She looked at the little frail lady, and said simply, "Dear Mrs. Montague, I think the root of the whole matter lies in this. The Lord made us all one family. We are all brothers and sisters. The lowest woman is your sister and my sister. The man lying in the gutter is our brother. What should we do to help these members of our common family, who are not as well off as we are? We should share our last crust with them. You and I, but for God's grace in placing us in different surroundings, might be in their places. I think it is wicked, criminal neglect in us to ignore this fact."

"It is, it is," said Mrs. Montague in a despairing voice. "I can't help feeling it. Tell me something I can do to help someone else."

Mrs. Morris sank back in her chair, her face very sad, and yet with something like pleasure in her eyes as she looked at her caller. "Your washerwoman," she said, "has a drunken husband and a crippled boy. I have often seen her standing over her tub, washing your delicate muslins and laces, and dropping tears into the water."

"I will never send her anything more—she shall not be

troubled," said Mrs. Montague hastily.

Mrs. Morris could not help smiling. "I have not made myself clear. It is not the washing that troubles her. It is her husband and the boy who worry her. If you and I take our work from her, she will have that much less money to depend upon, and will suffer in consequence. She is a hard-working and capable woman, and makes a fair living. I would not advise you to give her money, for her husband would find out and take it from her. But if you could visit her occasionally and show that you are interested in her, by talking or reading to her poor boy or showing him a picture book, you have no idea how grateful she would be to you, and how much it would cheer her on her hard, dreary way."

"I will go to see her tomorrow," said Mrs. Montague. "Can you think of anyone else I could visit?"

"A great many," said Mrs. Morris; "but I don't think you had better undertake too much at once. I will give you the addresses of three or four poor families, where an occasional visit would do untold good. That is, it will do them good if you treat them as you do your richer friends. Don't give them too much money, or too many presents, till you find out what they need. Try to feel interested in them. Find out their ways of living and what they want for their children, and help to get situations for them if you can. And be sure to remember that poverty does not always take away one's self-respect."

"I will, I will," said Mrs. Montague eagerly. "When can you give me these addresses?"

Mrs. Morris smiled again and, taking a piece of paper and a pencil from her workbasket, she wrote a few lines and handed them to Mrs. Montague.

The lady got up to take her leave. "And in regard to the

dog," said Mrs. Morris, following her to the door, "if you decide to allow Charlie to have one, you had better let him come in and have a talk with my boys about it. They seem to know all the dogs that are for sale in the town."

"Thank you. I shall be most happy to do so. He shall have his dog. When can you have him?"

"Tomorrow, the next day, any day at all. It makes no difference to me. Let him spend an afternoon and evening with the boys, if you do not object."

"It will give me much pleasure." The little lady bowed and smiled and, after stooping down to pat me, she tripped down the steps, got into her carriage, and drove away.

Mrs. Morris stood looking after her with a beaming face, and I began to think that I should like Mrs. Montague, too, if I knew her long enough. Two days later I was quite sure I should, for I had proof that she really liked me. When her little boy Charlie came to the house, he brought something for me done up in white paper. Mrs. Morris opened it, and there was a handsome, nickel-plated collar, with my name on it— *Beautiful Joe.*

Wasn't I pleased? They took off the shabby leather strap that the boys had given me when I came, and fastened on my new collar, and then Mrs. Morris held me up to a glass to look at myself. I felt so happy. Up to this time I had felt a little ashamed of my cropped ears and docked tail, but now that I had a fine new collar I could hold up my head with any dog.

"Dear old Joe," said Mrs. Morris, pressing my head tightly between her hands.

"You did a good thing the other day in helping me to start that little woman out of her selfish way of living."

I did not know about that, but I knew I felt very grateful

to Mrs. Montague for my new collar. Ever afterward when I met her in the street I stopped and looked at her. Sometimes she saw me and stopped her carriage to speak to me. I always wagged my tail, or rather my body, for I had no tail to wag, whenever I saw her, whether she saw me or not.

Her son got a beautiful Irish setter, called "Brisk." He had a silky coat and soft brown eyes, and his young master seemed very fond of him.

6

The Fox Terrier Billy

WHEN I came to the Morrises, I knew nothing about the proper way of bringing up a puppy. I once heard of a little boy whose sister beat him so much that he said he was brought up by hand. So I think, as Jenkins kicked me so much every day, I may say that I was brought up by foot.

Shortly after my arrival in my new home, I had a chance of seeing how one should bring up a puppy.

One day I was sitting beside Miss Laura in the parlor, when the door opened and Jack came in. One of his hands was laid over the other, and he said to his sister, "Guess what I've got here."

"A bird," she said.

"No."

"A rat."

"No."

"A mouse."

"No—a pup."

"Oh, Jack," she said reprovingly, for she thought he was telling a story.

He opened his hands, and there lay the tiniest morsel of a fox terrier puppy that I ever saw. He was white, with black and tan markings. His body was pure white, his tail black with a dash of tan, his ears black, and his face evenly marked with black and tan. We could not tell the color of his eyes, as they were not open. Later on, they turned out to be a pretty brown. His nose was pale pink. When he got older, it became jet black.

"Why, Jack!" exclaimed Miss Laura. "His eyes aren't open! Why did you take him from his mother?"

"She's dead," said Jack. "Left her pups to run about the yard for a little exercise. She found a piece of poisoned meat that some brute had thrown there, and she ate it. Four of her pups died, too. This is the only one left. Mr. Robinson says his man doesn't understand raising pups without their mothers, and he is going away, and he wants us to have it because we always have such good luck in nursing sick animals."

Mr. Robinson, I knew, was a friend of the Morrises, and a gentleman who was fond of fancy stock and imported a great deal of it from England. If this puppy came from him, it was sure to be a good one.

Miss Laura took the tiny creature and went upstairs thoughtfully. I followed her and watched her get a little basket and line it with cotton wool. She put the puppy in it and looked at him. Though it was midsummer and the house seemed very warm to me, the little creature was shivering, and making a low murmuring noise. She pulled the wool all over him and put the window down and set his basket in the sun.

Then she went to the kitchen and got some warm milk. She dipped her finger in it, and offered it to the puppy, but he wouldn't touch it. "Too young," Miss Laura said. She got a little piece of muslin, put some bread in it, tied a string round it, and dipped it in the milk. When she put this to the puppy's mouth, he sucked it greedily. He seemed starved, but Miss Laura let him have only a little.

Every few hours for the rest of the day she gave him some more milk, and I heard the boys say that for many nights she got up once or twice and heated milk over a lamp for him. One night the milk got cold before he took it, and he swelled up and became so ill that Miss Laura had to rouse her mother and get some hot water to plunge him in. That made him well again, and no one seemed to think it was a great deal of trouble to take for a creature that was nothing but a dog.

He fully repaid them for all his care, for he turned out to be one of the prettiest and most lovable dogs that I ever saw. They called him Billy, and the two events of his early life were the opening of his eyes and the swallowing of the muslin rag. The rag did not seem to hurt him. But Miss Laura said he had got so strong and so greedy that he must learn to eat like other dogs.

He was very amusing when he was a puppy. He was full of tricks, and he crept about in a mischievous way when one did not know he was near. He was a very small puppy and used to climb inside Miss Laura's jersey sleeve up to her shoulder when he was six weeks old. One day when the whole family was in the parlor, Mr. Morris suddenly flung aside his newspaper and began jumping up and down. Mrs. Morris was very much alarmed, and cried out, "My dear William, what is the matter?"

"There's a rat up my leg," he said, shaking it violently. Just then little Billy fell out on the floor and lay on his back looking up at Mr. Morris. He had felt cold and thought it would be warm inside Mr. Morris's trouser leg.

However, Billy never did any real mischief, thanks to Miss Laura's training. She began to punish him just as soon as he began to tear and worry things. The first thing he attacked was Mr. Morris's felt hat. The wind blew it down the hall one day, and Billy came along and began to try it with his teeth. I daresay it felt good to them, for a puppy is very much like a baby and loves something to bite.

Miss Laura found him, and he rolled his eyes at her quite innocently, not knowing that he was doing wrong. She took the hat away and, pointing from it to him, said, "Bad Billy!" Then she gave him two or three slaps with a bootlace. She never struck a little dog with her hand or a stick. She said clubs were for big dogs and switches for little dogs, if one had to use them. The best way was to scold, for a good dog feels a severe scolding as much as a whipping.

Billy was very much ashamed of himself. Nothing would induce him to look at a hat again. But he thought it was no harm to worry other things. He attacked one thing after another, the rugs on the floor, curtains, anything flying or fluttering, and Miss Laura patiently scolded him for each one, till at last it dawned upon him that he must not worry anything but a bone. So, finally, he got to be a very good dog.

There was one thing that Miss Laura was very particular about, and that was to have him fed regularly. We both got three meals a day. We were never allowed to go into the dining room, and while the family was at the table we lay in the hall outside and watched what was going on.

As soon as meals were over, Billy and I scampered after Miss Laura to the kitchen. We each had our own plate for food. Mary the cook often laughed at Miss Laura, because she would not let her dogs "dish" together. Miss Laura said that if she did, the larger one would get more than his share, and the little one would starve.

It was quite a sight to see Billy eat. He spread his legs apart to steady himself, and gobbled at his food like a duck. When he finished up, he always looked up for more, and Miss Laura would shake her head and say, "No, Billy; better longing than loathing. I believe that a great many little dogs are killed by overfeeding."

I must not forget to say that Billy was washed regularly— once a week with nice-smelling soap, and once a month with strong-smelling, disagreeable, carbolic soap. He had his own towels and wash cloths, and after being rubbed and scrubbed, he was rolled in a blanket and put by the fire to dry. Miss Laura said that a little dog that has been petted and kept in the house and has become tender, should never be washed and allowed to run about with a wet coat, unless the weather was very warm, for he would be sure to take cold.

I was more hardy than Billy, and so was Jim, the Morrises' spaniel. We took our baths in the sea. Every few days the boys took us down to the shore, and we went in swimming with them.

7

Training a Puppy

"NED, DEAR," said Miss Laura one day, "I wish you would train Billy to follow and retrieve. He is four months old now, and I shall soon want to take him out in the street."

"Very well, sister," said mischievous Ned. Catching up a stick, he said, "Come out to the garden, dogs."

Though he was brandishing his stick very fiercely, I was not at all afraid of him. As for Billy, he loved Ned.

The Morris garden was really not a garden, but a large piece of ground with the grass worn bare in many places, a few trees scattered about, and some raspberry and currant bushes along the fence. A lady who knew that Mr. Morris had not a large salary looked out of the dining-room window one day and said, "My dear Mrs. Morris, why don't you have this garden dug up? You could raise your own vegetables. It would be so much cheaper than buying them."

Mrs. Morris laughed in great amusement. "Think of the hens and cats and dogs and rabbits and, above all, the boys that I have. What sort of a garden would there be, and do you think it would be fair to take their playground away from them?"

The lady said no, she did not think it would be fair.

I am sure I don't know what the boys would have done without this strip of ground. Many a frolic and game they had there. In the present case, Ned walked around and around it with his stick on his shoulder, Billy and I strolling after him. Presently Billy made a dash aside to get a bone. Ned turned around and said firmly, "To heel!"

Billy looked at him innocently, not knowing in the least what he meant.

"To heel!" exclaimed Ned again. Billy thought he wanted to play and, putting his head on his paws, he began to bark. Ned laughed, but he kept saying, "To heel!" He would not say another word. He knew that if he said "Come here" or "Follow me" or "Go behind," it would only confuse Billy.

Finally, as Ned said the words over and over again and kept pointing to me, it seemed to dawn upon Billy that he wanted him to follow him. So he came beside me, and together we followed Ned around the garden, again and again.

Ned often looked behind with a pleased face, and I felt proud to think I was doing so well. But suddenly he turned and said, "Hie out!" Then I was dreadfully confused.

The Morrises all used the same words in training their dogs, and I had heard Miss Laura say this. But I had forgotten what it meant. "Good Joe," said Ned, turning around and patting me. "You have forgotten. I wonder where Jim is? He would help us."

He put his fingers in his mouth and blew a shrill whistle, and soon Jim came trotting up the lane from the street. He looked at us with his large, intelligent eyes, and wagged his tail slowly as if to say, "Well, what do you want of me?"

"Come and give me a hand at this training business, old Sobersides," said Ned with a laugh. "It's too slow to do it alone. Now, young gentlemen, attention! To heel!" He began to march around the garden again, and Jim and I followed closely at his heels while little Billy, seeing that he could not get us to play with him, came lagging behind.

Soon Ned turned around and said, "Hie out!" Jim sprang ahead and ran off in front as if he was after something. Now I remembered what "Hie out" meant! We were to have a lovely race wherever we liked. Little Billy loved this. We ran and scampered hither and thither.

After tea he called us out into the garden again and said he had something else to teach us. He turned up a tub on the wooden platform at the back door and sat on it, and then called Jim to him.

He took a small leather strap from his pocket. It had a nice strong smell. We all licked it, and each dog wished to have it. "No, Joe and Billy," said Ned, holding us both by our collars. "You wait a minute. Here, Jim."

Jim watched him very earnestly, and Ned threw the strap halfway across the garden and said, "Fetch it."

Jim never moved till he heard the words, "Fetch it." Then he ran swiftly, brought the strap, and dropped it in Ned's hand. Ned sent him after it two or three times. Then he said to

Jim, "Lie down," and turned to me. "Here, Joe, it is your turn."

He threw the strap under the raspberry bushes. Then he looked at me and said, "Fetch it." I knew quite well what he meant and ran joyfully after it. I soon found it by the strong smell, but the queerest thing happened when I got it in my mouth. I began to gnaw it and play with it, and when Ned called out, "Fetch it," I dropped it and ran toward him. I was not obstinate, but I was stupid.

Ned pointed to the place where it was, and spread out his empty hands. That helped me, and I ran quickly and got it. He made me get it for him several times. Sometimes I could not find it, and sometimes I dropped it; but he never stirred. He sat still till I brought it to him.

After a while he tried Billy, but it soon got dark and we could not see. So he took Billy and went into the house.

I stayed out with Jim for a while, and he asked me if I knew why Ned had thrown a strap for us instead of a bone or something hard.

Of course I did not know, and so Jim told me it was on his account. He was a bird dog and was never allowed to carry anything in his mouth, because it would make him hard-mouthed, and he would be apt to bite the birds when he was bringing them back to any person who was shooting with him. He said that he had been so carefully trained that he could even carry three eggs at a time in his mouth.

I said to him, "Jim, how is it that you never go out shooting? I have always heard that you were a dog for that, and yet you never leave home."

He hung his head a little and said he did not wish to go. Then, because he was an honest dog, Jim gave me the true reason.

8

A Ruined Dog

I WAS A sporting dog," he said bitterly, "for the first three years of my life. I belonged to a man who keeps a livery stable here in Fairport, and he used to hire me out to shooting parties.

"I was a favorite with all the gentlemen. I was crazy with delight when I saw the guns brought out, and would jump up and bite at them. I loved to chase birds and rabbits, and even now when the pigeons come near me, I tremble all over and have to turn away lest I should seize them. I often used to be in the woods from morning till night. I liked to have a hard search for a bird after it had been shot, and to be praised for bringing it out without biting or injuring it.

"I never got lost, for I am one of those dogs that can always tell where human beings are. I did not smell them. I would be too far away for that, but if my master was standing in some place and I took a long round through the woods, I knew exactly where he was and could make a shortcut back to him without returning in my tracks.

"But I must tell you about my trouble. One Sunday afternoon a party of young men came to get me. They had a dog with them, a cocker spaniel called Bob, but they wanted another. For some reason or other, my master was very unwilling to have me go. However, he at last consented, and they put me in the back of the wagon with Bob and the lunch baskets, and we drove off into the country.

"This Bob was a happy, merry-looking dog, and as we went along, he told me of the fine time we should have next day. The young men would shoot a little, and then they would get out their baskets and have something to eat, and would play cards and go to sleep under the trees, and we would be able to help ourselves to legs and wings of chickens, and anything we liked from the baskets.

"I did not like this at all. I was used to working hard through the week, and I liked to spend my Sundays quietly at home. However, I said nothing.

"That night we slept at a country hotel, and drove the next morning to the banks of a small lake where the young men were told there would be plenty of wild ducks. They were in no hurry to begin their sport. They sat down in the sun on some flat rocks at the water's edge and began to laugh and joke. Then they got mischievous, and seemed to forget all about their shooting. One of them, a rowdy if ever I saw one, proposed to have some fun with the dogs. They tied us both to a tree and, throwing a stick into the water, told us to get it.

Of course we struggled and tried to get free, and chafed our necks with the rope.

"Then one of them said that he believed I was gun-shy and, getting his gun, he said he was going to try me.

"He loaded the gun, and went to a little distance, and was ready to fire when the young man who owned Bob said he wasn't going to have his dog's legs shot off. He unfastened Bob and took him away. You can imagine my feelings, as I stood there tied to the tree, with that thoughtless stranger pointing his gun directly at me. He fired close to me a number of times—over my head and under my body. The earth was cut up all around me. I was terribly frightened and howled and begged to be freed.

"The other young men, who were sitting laughing at me, thought it was such good fun that they got their guns, too. I never wish to spend such a terrible hour again. I was sure they would kill me. Why, oh, why do some human beings find the sight of misery so mirth-provoking?

"Poor Bob, who was almost as frightened as I was, and who lay shivering under the wagon, was killed by a stray shot from his master's own gun. He gave one loud howl, kicked convulsively, then turned over on his side and lay quite still. This brought the young men to their senses. They were not bad young men. I suppose when they were little boys, they tied tin cans to puppies' tails and pulled the wings off butterflies. They probably never realized how cruel they were being.

"I was never the same dog again. I was quite deaf in my right ear, and though I strove against it, I was so terribly afraid of even the sight of a gun that I would run and hide myself whenever one was shown to me. My master was very angry with those young men, and it seemed as if he could not bear the sight of me. One day he took me very kindly and brought me here, and asked Mr. Morris if he did not want a good-natured dog to play with the children.

"I have a happy home here and I love the Morris boys. But I often wish I could keep from putting my tail between my legs and running home when I hear the sound of a gun."

"Never mind that, Jim," I said. "You should not fret over a thing for which you are not to blame. And I am sure you must be glad for one reason that you have left your old life."

"What is that?" he said.

"On account of the birds. You know Miss Laura thinks it is very wrong to kill the pretty creatures that fly about in the woods."

"So it is," he said, "unless one kills them at once. I have often felt angry with men for only half killing a bird. Have you ever had a good run in the woods, Joe?"

"No, never," I said.

"Some day I will take you. But now it is late and I must go to bed. Are you going to sleep in the kennel with me, or in the stable?"

"I think I will sleep with you, Jim. Dogs like company, you know, as well as human beings." I curled up in the straw beside him, and soon we were fast asleep.

I have known a good many dogs, but I don't think I ever saw such a good one as Jim. He was gentle and kind, and so sensitive that a hard word hurt him more than a blow. He was a great pet with Mrs. Morris, and as he had been so well trained, he was able to make himself very useful to her.

When she went shopping, he often carried a parcel in his mouth for her. He would never drop it or leave it anywhere. One day, she dropped her purse without knowing it, and Jim picked it up and brought it home in his mouth. She did not notice him, for he always walked behind her. When she got to her own door, she missed the purse. Turning around, she saw it in Jim's mouth.

Another day, a lady gave Jack Morris a canary cage as a present for Carl. He was bringing it home, when one of the little seed boxes fell out. Jim picked it up and carried it a long way before Jack discovered it.

9

The Parrot Bella

I OFTEN used to hear the Morrises speak about vessels that ran between Fairport and a place called the West Indies, carrying cargoes of lumber and fish, and bringing home molasses, spices, fruit, and other things. On one of the vessels, called the *Mary Jane,* was a cabin boy who was a friend of the Morris boys and often brought them presents from his voyages. The boys looked forward to seeing their friend.

One day, after I had been with the Morrises for some months, this boy arrived at the house with a bunch of green bananas in one hand and a parrot in the other. The boys were delighted with the parrot, and called their mother to see what a pretty bird she was.

Mrs. Morris seemed very much touched by the boy's

thoughtfulness in bringing a present such a long distance to her
sons, and thanked him warmly. The cabin boy became very
shy, and Mrs. Morris smiled and left him with the boys. I think
that she thought he would be more comfortable with them.

Jack put me up on the table to look at the parrot. The boy
held her by a string tied around one of her legs. She was a
gray parrot with a few red feathers in her tail, and she had
bright eyes and a very knowing air.

The boy said he had been careful to buy a young one that
could not speak, for he knew the Morris boys would not want
one chattering foreign gibberish, nor yet one that would
swear. He had kept her in his bunk in the ship, and had spent
all his leisure time in teaching her to talk. Then he looked at
her anxiously and said, "Come now! Show off, can't ye?"

I didn't know what he meant by all this, until afterward. I
had never heard of such a thing as birds talking. I stood on
the table staring hard at her, and she stared hard at me. I was
just thinking that I would not like to have her sharp little
beak fastened in my skin, when I heard someone say, "Beautiful Joe."

The voice seemed to come from the room, but I knew all
the voices there, and this was one I had never heard before.
So I thought I must be mistaken, and it was someone in the
hall. I struggled to get away from Jack to run and see who it
was. But he held me fast, and laughed with all his might. I
looked at the other boys and they were laughing, too.

Presently I heard again, "Beautiful Joe, Beautiful Joe."
The sound was close by, and yet it did not come from the cabin
boy, for he was all doubled up laughing, his face as red as a
beet.

"It's the parrot, Joe!" cried Ned. "Look at her, you gaby."

I did look at her, and with her head on one side, and the sauciest air in the world, she was saying, "Beau-ti-ful Joe, Beau-ti-ful Joe!"

I had never heard a bird talk before, and I felt so sheepish that I tried to get down and hide myself under the table. Then she began to laugh at me. "Ha, ha, ha, good dog—sic'em, boy. Rats, rats! Beau-ti-ful Joe, Beau-ti-ful Joe," she cried, rattling off the words as fast as she could.

I never felt so queer before in my life, and the boys were just roaring with delight at my puzzled face. Then the parrot began calling for Jim. "Where's Jim, where's good old Jim? Poor old dog. Give him a bone."

The boys brought Jim in the parlor, and when he heard her funny little cracked voice calling him, he nearly went crazy. "Jimmy, Jimmy, James Augustus!" she said, which was Jim's long name.

He made a dash out of the room, and the boys screamed so that Mr. Morris came down from his study to see what the noise meant. As soon as the parrot saw him, she would not utter another word. The boys told him, though, what she had been saying, and he seemed much amused to think that the cabin boy should have remembered so many sayings his boys made use of, and taught them to the parrot.

"Clever Polly," he said kindly. "Good Polly."

The cabin boy looked at him shyly, and Jack, who was a very sharp boy, said quickly, "Is not that what you call her, Henry?"

"No," said the boy. "I call her Bell, short for Bellzebub."

"I beg your pardon," said Jack very politely.

"Bell—short for Bellzebub," repeated the boy. "Ye see, I thought ye'd like a name from the Bible, bein' a minister's sons. I hadn't my Bible with me on this cruise, and I couldn't think of any girl's name out of it but Eve or Queen of Sheba, and they didn't seem very fit. So I asked one of me mates, an' he says for his part he guessed Bellzebub was as pretty a girl's name as any, so I give her that. 'Twould 'a' been better to let you name her, but ye see 'twouldn't 'a' been handy not to call her somethin', where I was teachin' her every day.''

Jack turned away and walked to the window, his face a deep scarlet. I heard him mutter, "Beelzebub, prince of devils," and so I suppose the cabin boy had given his bird a bad name.

Mr. Morris looked kindly at the cabin boy. "Do you ever call the parrot by her whole name?"

"No, sir," he replied. "I always call her Bell, but she calls herself Bella."

"Bella," repeated Mr. Morris. "That is a very pretty name. If you keep her, boys, I think you had better stick to that."

"Yes, Father," they all said. Then Mr. Morris started to go back to his study. On the doorsill, he paused to ask the cabin boy when his ship sailed. Finding that it was to be in a few days, he took out his pocketbook and wrote something in it. The next day he asked Jack to go to town with him, and when they came home, Jack said that his father had bought an oilskin coat for Henry Smith, and a handsome Bible, in which they were all to write their names.

After Mr. Morris left the room, the door opened and Miss Laura came in. She knew nothing about the parrot and was very much surprised to see it. Seating herself at the table, she held out her hands to it. She was so fond of pets of all kinds that she never thought of being afraid of them. At the same time, she never laid her hand suddenly on any animal. She held out her fingers and talked gently, so that if it wished to

come to her, it could. She looked at the parrot as if she loved
it, and the queer little thing walked right up and nestled its
head against the lace in the front of her dress.

"Pretty lady," the parrot said in a cracked whisper. "Give
Bella a kiss."

The boys were so pleased with this and set up such a shout
that their mother came into the room and said they had better
take the parrot out to the stable. Bella seemed to enjoy the
fun. "Come on, boys," she screamed, as Henry Smith lifted her
on his finger. "Ha, ha, ha! Come on, let's have some fun!
Where's the guinea pig? Where's Davy, the rat? Where's
pussy? Pussy, pussy, come here."

I followed her out to the stable and stayed there until
she noticed me and screamed out, "Ha, Joe! Beautiful Joe!
Where's your tail? Who cut your ears off?"

I don't think it was kind of the cabin boy to teach her this,
and I think she knew it teased me, for she said it over and
over again, and laughed and chuckled with delight. I left her
and did not see her till the next day when the boys had got a
fine large cage for her.

The place for her cage was by one of the hall windows, but
everybody in the house got so fond of her that she was moved
about from one room to another.

She hated her cage, and used to put her head close to the
bars and plead, "Let Bella out. Bella will be a good girl. Bella
won't run away."

After a time the Morrises did let her out, and she kept her
word and never tried to get away. Jack put a little handle on
her cage so that she could open and shut it herself. It was very
amusing to hear her say in the morning, "Clear the track,
children! Bella's going to take a walk," and see her turn the

handle with her claw and come out into the room. She was a very clever bird, and as she was petted and talked to a great deal, she learned many, many more words than the cabin boy had taught her. Soon she was a great favorite with family and pets alike, and took her place among them.

IO

Billy's Training Continued

WHEN BILLY was five months old, he had his first walk in the street. Miss Laura knew that he had been well trained, and so she did not hesitate to take him into town. She was not the kind of a young lady to go into the street with a dog that would not behave himself, and she was never willing to attract attention to herself by calling out orders to any of her pets.

As soon as we got down the front steps, she said quietly to Billy, "To heel." It was very hard for little, playful Billy to keep close to her, when he saw so many new and wonderful things about him. He had got acquainted with everything in the house and garden, but this outside world was full of things he wanted to look at and smell, and he was fairly crazy to play with some of the pretty dogs he saw running about. But he did just as he was told.

Soon we came to a shop, and Miss Laura went in to buy some ribbons. She said to me, "Stay out." But Billy she took in with her. I watched them through the glass door and saw her go to a counter and sit down. Billy stood behind her till she said, "Lie down." Then he curled himself at her feet. Some time later when she said, "Up," he sprang up and followed her out to the street.

Looking pleased, she took us to a shop where we both lay beside the counter. When we heard her ask the clerk for solid rubber balls, we could scarcely keep still. We both knew what "ball" meant.

She did not do any more shopping, but turned her face toward the sea. She was going to give us a nice walk along the beach. She walked along, the high wind blowing her cloak and dress about, and when we got past the houses, she had a little run with us.

We jumped and frisked and barked till we were tired, and then we walked quietly along.

A little distance ahead of us were some boys throwing sticks into the water for two Newfoundland dogs. Suddenly a quarrel sprang up between the dogs. They were both powerful creatures, and fairly matched in size. It was terrible to hear their fierce growling, and to see the way in which they tore at each other's throats. I looked at Miss Laura. If she had said a word, I would have run in and helped the dog that was getting the worst of it. But she told me to keep back, and ran on herself.

The boys were throwing water on the dogs and pulling their tails and hurling stones at them, but they could not separate them. Their heads seemed locked together, and they went back and forth over the stones, the boys crowding around them, shouting and beating and kicking and pulling at them.

"Stand back, boys," said Miss Laura. "I'll stop them." She pulled a little parcel from her purse, bent over the dogs, scattered a powder on their noses, and the next instant, the dogs were yards apart, nearly sneezing their heads off.

"I say, missis, what did you do? What's that stuff? Whew, it's pepper!" the boys exclaimed.

Miss Laura sat down on a flat rock and looked at them with a very pale face. "Oh, boys!" she said. "Why did you make those dogs fight? It is so cruel. They were playing happily till you set them on each other. Just see how they have torn their handsome coats."

" 'Tain't my fault," said one of the lads sullenly. "Jim Jones there said his dog could lick my dog, and I said he couldn't—and he couldn't, neither."

"Yes, he could," cried the other boy. "And if you say he couldn't, I'll smash your head."

The two boys began sidling up to each other with clenched fists. A third boy, who had a mischievous face, seized the paper that had held the pepper. Running up to them, he shook it in their faces.

There was enough pepper left to put all thoughts of fighting out of their heads. They began to cough and choke and splutter, and finally found themselves beside the dogs, where the four of them had a lively time.

The other boys yelled with delight and pointed fingers at them. "A sneezing concert! Ha, ha, ha!"

Miss Laura laughed, too, and even Billy and I curled up our lips. After a while they sobered down, and then, finding that the boys hadn't a handkerchief between them, Miss Laura took her own soft one, dipped it in a spring of fresh water nearby, and gave it to the two sneezers to wipe their red eyes.

Their ill humor had gone. When she turned to leave them, she said coaxingly, "You won't make those dogs fight any more, will you?"

"No, sirree, Bob," they answered.

Miss Laura went slowly home, and ever afterward when she met those boys, they called her "Miss Pepper."

When we got home we found Willie curled up by the window in the hall, reading a book. Miss Laura went to him and laid her hand on his shoulder. She said, "I was going to give the dogs a game of ball, but I'm rather tired."

Willie buried his nose a little farther in his book. "Gammon and spinach," he growled. "You're always tired."

Miss Laura sat down. She began to tell him about the dog fight. The book slipped to the floor. When she finished he said, "Bully for you, sister. Go now and rest yourself." Then, snatching the balls from her, he called to us and ran down to the basement.

We had a grand game with Willie. Miss Laura had trained us to do all kinds of things with balls—jumping for them, playing hide-and-seek, and catching them.

Billy could do more things than I could. He did one thing which I thought was very clever. He played ball by himself. He was so crazy about ball play that he could never get enough of it. Sometimes he rolled the ball over the floor, and sometimes he threw it in the air, and sometimes he pushed it through the staircase railings to the hall below. He always listened till he heard it drop, then he ran down and brought it back and pushed it through again.

We both had been taught a number of tricks. We could

sneeze and cough, and play dead, and say our prayers, and stand on our heads.

When anyone came in and Miss Laura had us show off any of our tricks, the remark was always, "What clever dogs. They are not like other dogs."

That was a mistake. Billy and I were not any brighter than many a miserable cur that skulked about the streets of Fairport. It was kindness and patience that did it all. When I was with Jenkins, he thought I was a very stupid dog. He would have laughed at the idea of anyone teaching me anything. But I was only sullen and obstinate because I was kicked about so much. If he had been kind to me, I would have done anything for him.

I loved to wait on Miss Laura and Mrs. Morris, and they taught both Billy and me to make ourselves useful about the house. Mrs. Morris didn't like going up and down the three long staircases, and sometimes we just raced up and down, waiting on her.

How often I have heard her go into the hall and say, "Please send me down a clean duster, Laura. Joe, you get it." I would run gaily up the steps, and then would come Billy's turn. "Billy, I have forgotten my keys. Go get them for me."

After a time we began to know the names of different articles and where they were kept, and we could get them ourselves. On sweeping days we worked very hard and enjoyed the fun. If Mrs. Morris was too far away to call to Mary for what she wanted, she wrote the name on a piece of paper, and told us to take it to her.

I must say a word about Billy's tail before I close this chapter. It is the custom to cut the ends of fox terriers' tails, but leave their ears untouched. Billy came to Miss Laura so young that his tail had not been cut off, and she would not have it done.

One day Mr. Robinson came in to see him, and he said, "You have made a fine-looking dog of him, but his appearance is ruined by the length of his tail."

"Mr. Robinson," said Mrs. Morris, patting little Billy who lay on her lap, "don't you think this little dog has a beautifully proportioned body?"

"Yes, I do," said the gentleman. "His points are all correct, save that one."

"But," she said, "if our Creator made that beautiful little body, don't you think he is wise enough to know what length of tail would be in proportion to it?"

Mr. Robinson would not answer her. He only laughed and said he thought she and Miss Laura were "cranks."

II

Goldfish and Canaries

THE MORRIS boys were all different. Jack was bright and clever, Ned was a wag, Willie was a bookworm, and Carl was a born trader.

Carl was always exchanging toys and books with his schoolmates, and they never got the better of him in a bargain. He said that when he grew up he was going to be a merchant, and he had already begun to carry on a trade in canaries and goldfish. He was very fond of what he called his "yellow pets," yet he never kept a pair of birds or a goldfish if he had a good offer for them from anyone in Fairport.

He slept alone in a large sunny room at the top of the house. By his own request, it was barely furnished, and there he raised his canaries and kept his goldfish.

He was not fond of having visitors to his room, because he said they frightened his canaries. After Mrs. Morris made his bed in the morning, the door was closed, and no one was supposed to go in till he came from school. Once Billy and I followed him upstairs without his knowing it, but as soon as he saw us he sent us down again in a great hurry.

One day Bella walked into his room to inspect the canaries. She was quite a spoiled bird by this time, and I heard Carl telling the family afterward that it was as good as a play to see Miss Bella strutting in with her breast stuck out, and her conceited little air, and to hear her say shrilly, "Good morning, birds, good morning! How do you do, Carl? Glad to see you, boy."

"Well, I'm not glad to see you," he said decidedly. "And don't you ever come up here again! You'd frighten my canaries to death." And he sent her flying downstairs.

How cross she was! She came shrieking to Miss Laura. "Bella loves birds. Bella wouldn't hurt birds. Carl's bad."

Miss Laura petted and soothed her, telling her to go find Davy and he would play with her. Bella and the rat were great friends. It was very funny to see them going about the house together. From the very first she had liked him and coaxed him into her cage, where he soon became quite at home—so much so that he always slept there. About nine o'clock every evening if he was not with her, she went all over the house crying, "Davy! Davy! Time to go to bed. Come sleep in Bella's cage."

He was very fond of the nice sweet cakes she got to eat, but she never could get him to eat coffee grounds—the food she liked best.

Miss Laura spoke to Carl about Bella, and told him he had

hurt her feelings, and so he petted her a little to make up for it. Then his mother told him that she thought he was making a mistake to keep his canaries so much to themselves. They had become so timid that when she went into the room they were uneasy till she left it. She told him that petted birds or animals are sociable and like company, unless they are kept by themselves, when they become shy. She advised him to let other boys go into the room, and occasionally to bring some of his pretty singers downstairs, where all the family could enjoy seeing and hearing them, and where the birds could get used to seeing other people besides himself.

Carl looked thoughtful, and his mother went on to say that there was no one in the house, not even the cat, that would harm his birds.

"You might even charge admission for a day or two," said Jack gravely. "Introduce us to the canaries and make a little money."

Carl was rather annoyed at this, but his mother calmed him by showing him a letter she had just received from one of her brothers, asking her to let one of her boys spend his Christmas holidays in the country with him.

"I want you to go, Carl," she said.

He was very much pleased, but he looked sober when he thought of his pets.

"Laura and I will take care of them," said his mother, "and start the new management of them."

"Very well," said Carl. "I will go, then. I've no young ones now, so you will not find them much trouble."

I thought it was a great deal of trouble to take care of them. The first morning after Carl left, Billy and Bella and Davy and I followed Miss Laura upstairs. She made us sit in a row by the door, lest we should startle the canaries.

She had a great many things to do. First, the canaries had their baths. They had to get them at the same time every morning. Miss Laura filled the little white dishes with water and put them in the cages, and then came and sat on a stool by the door. Bella and Billy and Davy climbed into her lap, and I stood close by her.

It was so funny to watch those canaries. They put their heads on one side and looked first at their little baths and then at us. They knew we were strangers. Finally, as we were all very quiet, they got into the water; and what a good time they had, fluttering their wings and splashing, and cleaning themselves so nicely.

Then they got up on their perches and sat in the sun, shaking themselves and picking at their feathers.

Miss Laura cleaned each cage, and gave each bird some mixed rape and canary seed. I heard Carl tell her before he left not to give them much hemp seed, for that was too fattening. He was very careful about their food. During the summer I had often seen him taking up nice green things to them —celery, chickweed, tender cabbage, peaches, apples, pears, bananas. And now, at Christmas time, he had green stuff growing in small pots along the window ledge.

Besides that he gave them crumbs of coarse bread, crackers, lumps of sugar, cuttlefish to peck at, and a number of other things. Miss Laura did everything just as he told her, but I think she talked to the birds more than he did. She was very particular about their drinking water, and washed out the little glass cups that held it most carefully.

After the canaries were clean and comfortable, Miss Laura set their cages in the sun and turned to the goldfish. They were in large glass globes on the window seat. She cleaned each globe and scattered wafers of fish food on top of the fresh water. Then her work was finished for another morning.

She went away for a while, but every few hours through the day she ran up to Carl's room to see how the fish and canaries were getting on. If the room was too chilly she turned on more heat, but she did not keep it too warm, for that would make the birds tender.

After a time the canaries got to know her, and they hopped gaily around their cages and chirped and sang whenever they saw her coming. Then she began to take some of them downstairs, and to let them out of their cages for an hour or so every day. They were very happy little creatures, and chased each other about the room. Sometimes they lit on Miss Laura's head and pecked saucily at her face as she sat sewing and watching them. They were not at all afraid of me nor of Billy, and it was quite a sight to see them hopping up to Bella. She looked so large beside the little canaries.

One day just after Carl got back home, Mrs. Montague drove up to the house with a canary cage carefully done up in a shawl. She said that a bad-tempered housemaid, in cleaning the cage that morning, had become angry with the bird and struck it, breaking its leg. She was very much annoyed with the girl for her cruelty and had dismissed her, and now she wanted Carl to take her bird and nurse it and try to heal the broken leg.

Carl had just come in from school. He threw down his books, took the shawl from the cage, and looked in. The poor little canary was sitting in a corner. Its eyes were half shut, one leg hung loose.

Carl was very much interested in it. He asked Mrs. Montague to help him, and together they split matches and tore up strips of muslin, and bandaged the broken leg. He put the little bird back in the cage, and it seemed more comfortable. "I think he will do now," he said to Mrs. Montague. "But do you want to leave him with me for a few days?"

She gladly agreed to this and went away, after telling him that the bird's name was Dick.

The next morning at the breakfast table, I heard Carl telling his mother that as soon as he woke up he sprang out of bed and went to see how the canary was. During the night poor foolish Dick had picked off the splints from his leg, and now it was as bad as ever.

"I shall have to perform a surgical operation," said Carl.

I did not know what he meant, and so I watched him when, after breakfast, he brought the bird down to his mother's room. She held it while he took a pair of sharp scissors and cut its leg right off a little way above the broken place. Then he put some Vaseline on the tiny stump, bound it up, and left the canary in his mother's care. All the morning as she sat sewing, she watched Dick to see that he did not pick the bandage away.

When Carl came home, Dick was so much better that he had managed to fly up on his perch and was eating seeds quite gaily.

"Poor Dick!" said Carl. "Leg and a stump!" Dick imitated him in a few little chirps. "A leg and a stump!"

"Why, he is saying it, too!" exclaimed Carl, and burst out laughing.

Dick seemed cheerful enough, but it was very pitiful to see him dragging his poor little stump around the cage, and resting it against the perch to keep him from falling. When

Mrs. Montague came the next day, she could not bear to look at him.

"Oh, dear!" she exclaimed. "I cannot take that disfigured bird home." I could not help thinking how different she was from Miss Laura, who loved any creature all the more if it had some blemish about it.

"What shall I do?" said Mrs. Montague. "I miss my little bird so much. I shall have to get a new one. Carl, will you sell me one?"

"I will *give* you one, Mrs. Montague," said the boy eagerly. "I would like to do so."

Mrs. Morris looked pleased to hear Carl say this. She sometimes was afraid that in his love for making money he would become selfish.

Mrs. Montague was very kind to the Morris family, and Carl seemed quite pleased to do her a favor. He took her up to his room and let her choose the bird she liked best. She took a handsome yellow one, called Barry. He was a good singer, and a great favorite of Carl's. The boy put him in the cage, wrapped it up well, for it was a cold, snowy day, and carried it out to Mrs. Montague's sleigh.

She gave him a pleasant smile and drove away, and Carl ran up the steps into the house.

"It's all right, Mother," he said, giving Mrs. Morris a hearty, boyish kiss, as she stood waiting for him. "I don't mind letting her have it."

"But you expected to sell that one, didn't you?" his mother asked.

"Mrs. Smith said maybe she'd take it when she came home from Boston, but I daresay she'd change her mind and get one there."

"How much were you going to ask for him?"

"Well, I wouldn't sell Barry for less than ten dollars, or rather, I wouldn't have sold him." And he ran out to the stable to join the other boys.

Mrs. Morris sat on the hall chair, patting me in a rather absentminded way as I rubbed against her. Then she got up and went into her husband's study, and told him what Carl had done.

Mr. Morris seemed very pleased to hear about it, but when his wife asked him to do something to make up the loss to the boy, he said, "I had rather not do that. To encourage a child to do a kind action, and then to reward him for it is not always a sound principle."

But Carl did not go without his reward. That evening Mrs. Montague's coachman brought a note to the house addressed to Mr. Carl Morris. He read it aloud to the family:

"My dear Carl: I am charmed with my little bird, and he has whispered to me one of the secrets of your room. You want fifteen dollars very much to buy something for it. I am sure you won't be offended with an old friend for supplying you the means to get this something.

"Ada Montague

"Just the thing for my stationary tank for the goldfish," exclaimed Carl. "I've wanted it for a long time; it isn't good to keep them in globes. But how in the world did she find out? I've never told anyone."

Mrs. Morris smiled and said, "Barry must have told her."

As for little lame Dick, Carl never sold him, and he became a family pet. His cage hung in the parlor, and from morning till night his cheerful voice was heard, chirping and singing as if he had not a trouble in the world. They took great care of him. He was never allowed to be too hot or too cold. Everybody gave him a cheerful word in passing his cage, and if his singing was too loud, they gave him a little mirror to look at himself in. He loved this mirror and often stood before it for an hour at a time.

12

Malta the Cat

THE FIRST time I had a good look at the Morris cat, I thought she was the queerest-looking animal I had ever seen. She was dark gray—just the color of a mouse. Her eyes were a yellowish green, and for the first few days I was at the Morrises' she looked very unkindly at me. Then she got over her dislike and we became very good friends. She was a beautiful cat, and so gentle and affectionate that the whole family loved her.

She was three years old, and she had come to Fairport in a vessel with some sailors, who had brought her from a faraway place. Her name was Malta, and she was a real Maltese cat.

She was a very knowing cat, and always came when she was called. Miss Laura used to wear a little silver whistle that she blew when she wanted any of her pets. It was a shrill whistle, and we could hear it a long way from home. I have seen her standing at the back door whistling for Malta, and the pretty creature's head would appear somewhere, always high up, for she was a great climber, and she would come running along the top of the fence, saying, "Meouw, meouw," in a funny, short way.

Mary, the cook, was very fond of cats, and used to keep Malta in the kitchen as much as she could, but nothing would make the cat stay down there if there was any music going on upstairs. The Morris pets were all fond of music. As soon as Miss Laura sat down to the piano to sing or play, we came from all parts of the house. Malta cried to get upstairs, Davy scampered through the hall, and Bella hurried after him. If I was outdoors I ran into the house, and Jim got on a box and looked through the window. We liked to hear Miss Laura play.

Malta had been so kindly treated that she never ran from anyone, except from strange dogs. She knew they would be likely to hurt her. If they came upon her suddenly, she faced them, and she was a pretty good fighter when she was put to it. I once saw her having a brush with a big mastiff that lived a few blocks from us, and giving him a good fright, which just served him right.

I was shut up in the parlor. Someone had closed the door, and I could not get out. I was watching Malta from the window as she daintily picked her way across the muddy street. She was such a soft, pretty, amiable-looking cat. She didn't look that way, though, when the mastiff rushed out of the alleyway at her.

She sprang back and glared at him like a fierce little tiger.

Her tail was enormous. Her eyes were like balls of fire, and she was spitting and snarling, as if to say, "If you touch me, I'll tear you to pieces!"

The dog, big as he was, did not dare attack her. He walked around and around her like a great, clumsy elephant, and she turned her small body as he turned his, and kept up a dreadful hissing and spitting. Suddenly I saw a spitz dog hurrying down the street. He was going to help the mastiff, and Malta would be badly hurt. I had barked and no one had come to let me out; so I sprang through the window.

Just then there was a change. Malta had seen the second dog, and she knew she must get rid of the mastiff. With an agile bound she sprang on his back and dug her sharp claws in, till he put his tail between his legs and ran up the street, howling with pain. She rode a little way, then sprang off and ran up the lane to the stable.

I was very angry and wanted to fight something; so I pitched into the spitz dog. He was a snarly, cross-grained creature, no friend to Jim and me, and he would have been only too glad of a chance to help kill Malta.

I gave him one of the worst beatings he ever had. I don't suppose it was right for me to do it, for Miss Laura says dogs should never fight; but he had worried Malta before, and he had no business to do it. She belonged to our family. Jim and I never worried *his* cat. I had been longing to give him a shaking for some time, and now I felt for his throat through his thick hair, and dragged him all around the street. Then I let him go, and he was a civil dog ever afterward.

Malta was very grateful, and licked a little place where the spitz bit me. I did not get scolded for the broken window. Mary had seen me from the kitchen window and told Mrs.

Morris that I had gone to help Malta.

Malta was a very wise cat. She knew quite well that she must not harm the parrot nor the canaries, and she never tried to catch them, even though she was left alone in the room with them.

I have seen her lying in the sun, blinking sleepily and listening with great pleasure to Dick's singing. Miss Laura even taught her not to hunt the birds outside.

One day Miss Laura stood at the window, looking into the garden. Malta was lying on the platform, staring at the sparrows that were picking up crumbs from the ground. She trembled and half rose every few minutes, as if to go after them. Then she lay down again. She was trying very hard not to creep on them. Presently a neighbor's cat came stealing along the fence, keeping one eye on Malta and the other on the sparrows. Malta was so angry! She sprang up and chased her away, and then came back to the platform, where she lay down again and waited for the sparrows to come back. For a long time she stayed there, and never once tried to catch them.

Miss Laura was very pleased. She went to the door and said softly, "Come here, Malta."

The cat put up her tail and, meouwing gently, came into the house. Miss Laura took her up in her arms and, going down to the kitchen, asked Mary to give her a saucer of her very sweetest milk for the best cat in the United States of America.

Malta got great praise for this, and I never knew of her catching a bird afterward. She was well fed in the house and had no need to hurt such harmless creatures.

She was very fond of her home, and never went far away, as Jim and I did. Once when Willie was going to spend a few weeks with a little friend who lived fifty miles from Fairport, he took it into his head that Malta should go with him. His mother told him that cats did not like to go away from home. But he said he would be good to her, and begged so hard to take her along with him that at last his mother consented.

He had been a few days in this place, when he wrote home to say that Malta had run away. She had seemed very unhappy, and though he had kept her with him all the time, she had acted as if she wanted to get away.

When the letter was read to Mr. Morris, he said, "Malta is on her way home. Cats have a wonderful cleverness in finding their way to their own dwelling. She will be very tired. Let us go and meet her."

Willie had gone to this place in a coach. Mr. Morris got a buggy and took Miss Laura and me with him, and we started out. We went slowly along the road. Every little while Miss Laura blew her whistle and called, "Malta! Malta!" And I barked as loudly as I could. Mr. Morris drove for several hours. Then we stopped at a house, had dinner, and set out again. We were going through a thick wood when I saw a small dark creature away ahead, trotting toward us. It was Malta. I gave a joyful bark, but she did not know me and plunged into the wood.

I ran in after her, barking and yelping, and Miss Laura blew her whistle as loudly as she could. Soon there was a little gray head peeping at us from the bushes, and Malta bounded out, gave me a look of surprise, and then leaped into the buggy to Miss Laura's lap.

Malta did not like dogs, but she was very good to cats. One day when there was no one about and the garden was very quiet, I saw her go stealing into the stable, and come out again, followed by a starved-looking cat that had been deserted by some people who lived in the next street. She led this cat to her catnip bed and watched her kindly while she rolled and rubbed herself in it. Then Malta had a roll in it herself, and they both went back to the stable.

Catnip is a favorite plant with cats, and Miss Laura always kept some of it growing for Malta.

For a long time this strange cat had a home in the stable. Malta carried her food every day, and after a time Miss Laura found out about her and did what she could to make her well. In time she got to be a strong, sturdy-looking cat, and Miss Laura got a home for her with an invalid lady.

It was nothing new for the Morrises to feed deserted cats. Some summers, Mrs. Morris said, she had a dozen to take care of. Careless and cruel people would go away for the summer, shutting up their houses and making no provision for the poor cats that had been allowed to sit snugly by the fire all winter. At last Mrs. Morris got into the habit of putting a little notice in the Fairport paper, asking people who were going away for the summer to provide for their cats during their absence.

13

The Beginning
of an Adventure

IT WAS on Saturday night a week before Christmas. We were having cold, frosty weather. The Morris family was sitting around the blazing fire in the parlor—Mrs. Morris sewing, the boys reading and studying, and Mr. Morris with his head buried in a newspaper. Billy and I lay on the floor at their feet.

I was feeling very drowsy and had almost dropped off to sleep, when Ned gave me a push with his foot. He was a great tease, and he delighted in getting me to make a simpleton of myself. I tried to keep my eyes on the fire, but I could not, and just had to turn and look at him.

He was holding his book up between himself and his

mother, and was opening his mouth as wide as he could and throwing back his head, pretending to howl.

For the life of me I could not help giving a loud howl. Mrs. Morris looked up from her sewing and said, "Bad Joe, keep still."

The boys were all laughing behind their books, for they knew what Ned was doing. Presently he started off again, and I was just beginning another howl that might have made Mrs. Morris send me out of the room, when the door opened and a young girl called Bessie Drury came in.

She had a cap on and a shawl thrown over her shoulders, and she had just run across the street from her father's house.

"Oh, Mrs. Morris," she said. "Will you let Laura come over and stay with me tonight? Mamma has just had a telegram from Bangor saying that her aunt, Mrs. Cole, is very ill, and she wants to see her, and Papa is going to take her there

by tonight's train, and she is afraid I will be lonely if I don't have Laura."

"Can you not come and spend the night here?" said Mrs. Morris.

"No, thank you. I think Mamma would rather have me stay in our house."

"Very well," said Mrs. Morris. "I think Laura would like to go."

"Yes, indeed," said Miss Laura, smiling at her friend. "I will come over in half an hour."

"Thank you so much," said Miss Bessie. She hurried away.

After she left, Mr. Morris looked up from his paper. "I hope there will be someone in the house besides those two girls."

"Oh, yes," said Mrs. Morris. "Mrs. Drury has her old nurse, who has been with her for twenty years, and there are two

maids besides, and Donald, the coachman, who sleeps over the stable. So they are well protected."

"Very good," said Mr. Morris, returning to his paper.

Of course, dumb animals do not understand all that they hear spoken of. But I think human beings would be astonished if they knew how much we can gather from their looks and voices. I knew that Mr. Morris did not quite like the idea of having his daughter go to the Drurys' when the master and mistress of the house were away, and so I made up my mind that I would go with her.

When she came downstairs with her little satchel on her arm, I got up and stood beside her.

"Dear old Joe," she said. "You must not come."

I pushed myself out the door beside her after she had kissed her mother and father and the boys.

"Go back, Joe," she said firmly.

I had to step back then, but I cried and whined, and she looked at me in astonishment. "I will be back in the morning, Joe," she said gently. "Don't squeal in that way." And she shut the door and went out.

I felt dreadful. I walked up and down the floor and ran to the window and howled without having to look at Ned.

Mr. Morris looked at me intently. He turned to his wife and said, "Mother, let the dog go."

"Very well," she said. "Jack, just run over with him, and tell Mrs. Drury how he is acting, and that I will be much obliged if she will let him stay all night with Laura."

The Drurys lived in a large white house with trees all around it and a garden at the back. They were rich people and had a great deal of company. Through the summer I had often seen carriages at the door, and ladies and gentlemen in light clothes walking over the lawn, and sometimes I smelled nice things they were having to eat. They did not keep any dogs, nor pets of any kind; so Jim and I never had an excuse to call there.

Jack and I were soon at the front door, and he rang the bell and gave me in charge of the maid who opened it. The girl listened to his message for Mrs. Drury. Then she walked upstairs, smiling and looking back at me over her shoulder.

I walked softly into a front room, and there I found my dear Miss Laura. Miss Bessie was with her, and they were cramming things into a portmanteau. They both ran out to find out how I came there, and just then a gentleman came hurriedly upstairs and said the cab had come for Mrs. Drury.

There was a scene of great confusion and hurry, but in a few minutes it was all over. The cab had rolled away, and the house was quiet.

"Nurse, you must be tired; you had better go to bed," said Miss Bessie, turning to the elderly woman as we all stood in the hall. "Susan, will you bring some supper to the dining room for Miss Morris and me? What will you have, Laura?"

"What are you going to have?" asked Miss Laura.

"Hot chocolate and tea biscuits."

"Then I will have the same."

"Bring some cake, too, Susan," said Miss Bessie, "and something for the dog. I daresay he would like some of that turkey that was left from dinner."

What fun we had over our supper! The two girls sat at the big dining table and sipped their chocolate and laughed and talked, and I had the skeleton of a whole turkey on a newspaper that Susan spread on the carpet.

I was very careful not to drag it about, and Miss Bessie

laughed at me till the tears came in her eyes.

"That dog is a gentleman," she said. "See how he holds the bones on the paper with his paws, and strips off the meat with his teeth. Oh, Joe, Joe, you are a funny dog! And you are having a funny supper. I have heard of quail on toast, but I never heard of turkey on newspaper."

"Hadn't we better go to bed?" said Miss Laura, when the hall clock struck eleven.

"Yes, I suppose we had," said Miss Bessie. "Where is this animal to sleep?"

"I don't know," said Miss Laura. "He sleeps in the stable at home, or in the kennel with Jim."

"Suppose Susan makes him a nice bed by the kitchen stove?" asked Miss Bessie.

Susan made the bed, but I was not willing to sleep in it. I barked so loudly when they shut me up alone, that they had to let me go upstairs with them.

Miss Laura was almost angry with me, but I could not help it. I had come over there to protect her, and I wasn't going to leave her if I could help it.

Miss Bessie had a handsomely furnished room, with a soft carpet on the floor and pretty curtains at the windows. There were two single beds in it, and the two girls dragged them close together, so that they could talk after they got in bed.

Before Miss Bessie put out the light, she told Miss Laura not to be alarmed if she heard anyone walking about in the night, for the nurse was sleeping across the hall from them, and she would probably come in once or twice to see if they were sleeping comfortably.

The two girls talked for a long time, and then they fell asleep. I was tired, and I had a very soft and pleasant bed on a fur rug near Miss Laura; so I soon fell into a heavy sleep. But I waked up at the slightest noise. Once Miss Laura turned in bed, and another time Miss Bessie laughed in her sleep, and again, there were queer crackling noises in the frosty limbs of the trees outside that made me start up quickly out of my sleep.

There was a big clock in the hall, and every time it struck I waked up. Once, just after it had struck some hour, I jumped up out of a sound sleep. I had been dreaming about my early home. Jenkins was after me with a whip, and my limbs were quivering and trembling as if I had been trying to get away from him.

I sprang up and shook myself. Then I took a turn around the room. The two girls were breathing gently; I could scarcely hear them. I walked to the door and looked into the hall. There was a dim light burning there. The door of the nurse's room stood open. I went quietly to it and looked in. She was breathing heavily and muttering in her sleep.

I went back to my rug and tried to go to sleep, but I could not. Such an uneasy feeling was upon me that I had to keep walking about. I went out to the hall again and stood at the head of the staircase. I thought I would take a walk through the lower hall, and then go to bed again.

The Drurys' carpets were all like velvet, and my paws did not make a rattling on them as they did on the oil cloth at the Morrises'. I crept down the stairs like a cat and walked along the lower hall, smelling under all the doors, listening as I went. There was no night light burning down here, and it was quite dark, but if there had been any strange person about I would have smelled him.

I was surprised when I got near the farther end of the hall

to see a tiny gleam of light shine for an instant from under the dining-room door. Then it went away again. The dining room was the place to eat. Surely none of the people in the house would be there at this time.

I went and sniffed under the door. There was a smell there. It smelled like Jenkins. It *was* Jenkins.

14

How We Caught the Burglar

I THOUGHT I would go crazy! I scratched at the door and barked and yelped. I sprang upon it, and though I was quite a heavy dog by this time, I felt as if I were as light as a feather.

Every few seconds I stopped and put my head down to the doorsill to listen. There was a rushing about inside the room, and a chair fell over, and someone seemed to be getting out of the window.

This made me worse than ever. I did not stop to think that I was only a medium-sized dog, and that Jenkins would probably kill me if he got his hands on me. I was so furious with him that I thought only of getting hold of him.

In the midst of the noise I made, there was a screaming and a rushing to and fro upstairs. I ran up and down the hall, and halfway up the steps and back again. I did not want Miss Laura to come down, but how was I to make her understand? There she was, in her white gown, leaning over the railing and holding back her long hair, her face a picture of surprise and alarm.

"The dog has gone mad," screamed Miss Bessie. "Nurse, pour a pitcher of water on him."

The nurse was more sensible. She ran downstairs, her night-cap flying and a blanket that she had seized from her bed trailing behind her.

"There are thieves in the house!" she shouted at the top of her voice. "The dog has found it out!"

She did not go near the dining-room door, but threw open the front one, crying, "Policeman! Policeman! Help, help, thieves, murder!"

Such a screaming as that old woman made! She was worse than I was. I dashed by her, out through the hall door and away down to the gate, where I heard someone running. I gave a few loud yelps to call Jim, and leaped the gate as the man before me had done.

There was something savage in me that night. I think it must have been the smell of Jenkins. I felt as if I could tear him to pieces. I was hunting him, as he had hunted my mother and me, and the thought gave me pleasure.

Old Jim soon caught up with me, and I gave him a push with my nose, to let him know I was glad he had come. We rushed swiftly on, and at the corner caught up with the man who was running away from us.

I gave an angry growl and, jumping up, I bit at his leg. He turned around, and though it was not a bright night, there was light enough for me to see the ugly face of my old master.

He caught up a handful of stones and threw them at us. Then, away in front of us, came a queer whistle, and then another one like it behind us. Jenkins made a strange noise in his throat and started to run down a side street, away from the direction of the two whistles.

I was afraid that he was going to get away, and though I could not hold him, I kept springing up on him and once I tripped him up. He kicked me against the side of a wall, and gave me two or three hard blows with a stick that he caught up, and kept throwing stones at me.

Soon Jenkins came to a high wall, where he stopped and, with a hurried look behind, began to climb over it. The wall was too high for me to jump. He was going to escape! I barked as loudly as I could for someone to come, and then sprang up and held him firmly by the leg as he was getting over.

I had such a grip that I went over the wall with him, and left Jim on the other side. Jenkins fell on his face in the earth. Then he got up and pounced upon me. Just then there was a running sound. Two men came down the street and sprang upon the wall, just where Jim was leaping up and down and barking in distress.

I saw at once by their uniforms and the clubs in their hands that they were policemen. In one short instant they had hold of Jenkins. He gave up then, but he snarled at me, "If it hadn't been for that cur, I'd never have been caught. Why—" And he staggered back. "If it isn't my own dog!"

"More shame to you," said one of the policemen sternly. "What have you been up to at this time of night, to have your own dog and a quiet minister's spaniel chasing you through the street?"

Jenkins would not tell them anything, and I could not. There was a house in the garden, and just at this minute someone opened a window and called out, "Hallo, there, what are you doing?"

"We're catching a thief, sir," said one of the policemen. "Leastwise I think that's what he's been up to. There's a woman at a house on Washington Street that's yelling blue murder."

Jenkins was handcuffed and then the policemen hurried him toward Washington Street. As we came near our house, we saw lights gleaming through the darkness, and heard people running to and fro. The nurse's shrieking had alarmed the neighborhood. The Morris boys were all out in the street, half clad and shivering with cold, and the Drurys' coachman was running about with a lantern.

The neighbors' houses were all lighted up, and a good many people were hanging out their windows and opening their doors and calling to each other to know what all this noise meant.

When the policemen appeared with Jenkins, and with Jim and me at their heels, quite a crowd gathered around to hear their story. What a fuss was made over us.

"Brave dogs!" everybody said. "Noble dogs!" How they patted and praised us. We were very proud and happy, and stood up and wagged our tails, at least Jim did, and I wagged what I could. Then they found out what a state we were in. Mrs. Morris cried and, catching me up in her arms, ran into the house with me, and Jack followed with old Jim. One policeman led Jenkins off to the lockup.

We all went into the parlor. There was a good fire there, and Miss Laura and Miss Bessie were sitting over it. They sprang up when they saw us, and right there in the parlor washed our wounds and made us lie down by the fire.

"You saved our silver, brave Joe," said Miss Bessie. "Just wait till my papa and mamma come home, and see what they will say. Well, Jack, what is the latest?" as the Morris boys came trooping into the room.

"The policeman has been questioning your nurse and examining the dining room, and has gone down to the station to make his report, and do you know what he has found out?" said Jack excitedly.

"No—what?" asked Miss Bessie.

"Why, that villain was going to burn your house."

Miss Bessie gave a little shriek. "Why, what do you mean?"

"Well," said Jack, "they think by what they discovered, that he planned to pack his bag with silver and carry it off. But just before he did so, he would pour oil around the room and set fire to it, so people would not find out that he had been robbing you."

"Why, we might all have been burned to death," said Miss Bessie. "He couldn't burn the dining room without setting fire to the rest of the house."

"Certainly not," said Jack. "That shows what a villain he is."

"Do you know this for certain, Jack?" asked Miss Laura.

"Well, they suppose so. They found some bottles of oil along with the bag he had for the silver."

"How horrible! You darling old Joe, perhaps you saved our lives!" And pretty Miss Bessie affectionately patted my ugly, swollen head.

The next day the Drurys came home, and everything was found out about Jenkins. The night they left Fairport he had been hanging about the station. He knew just who were left in the house, for he had once supplied them with milk, and knew all about their family. He had no customers at this time, for after Mr. Harry rescued me, and that piece came out in the paper about him, he found that no one would take milk from him.

He was therefore ready for any kind of mischief that turned up, and when he saw the Drurys going away in the train, he thought he would steal a bag of silver from the sideboard, then set fire to the house and run away and hide the silver. After a time he would take it to some city and sell it.

He was made to confess all this. Then for his wickedness he was sent to prison for ten years, and I hope he will get to be a better man there, and be one after he comes out.

One day Mrs. Drury came over to see me.

"Mrs. Morris," she said, "I shall feel eternally grateful to Joe for saving not only our property—for that is a trifle—but my darling daughter from fright and annoyance, and a possible injury or loss of life. How can I make him understand that?"

"I think he understands," said Mrs. Morris. "He is a very wise dog." And smiling in great amusement, she called me to her and put my paws on her lap. "Look at Mrs. Drury, Joe. She is pleased with you for driving Jenkins away from her house. You remember Jenkins?"

I barked angrily and limped to the window.

"How intelligent he is!" said Mrs. Drury. "My husband has sent to New York for a watchdog, and he says that from now on our house shall never be without one. Now I must go. Your dog is happy, Mrs. Morris, and I can do nothing for him, except to say that I shall never forget him, and I wish he would come over occasionally to see us. Perhaps when we get our dog, he will. I shall tell my cook whenever she sees him to give him something to eat.

"This is a souvenir for Laura of that dreadful night. I feel under a deep obligation to you, and so I am sure you will allow her to accept it." Then she gave Mrs. Morris a little box and went away.

When Miss Laura came in, she opened the box, and found in it a handsome diamond ring. On the inside of it was engraved: "Laura, in memory of December 20, 18—. From her grateful friend, Bessie."

The diamond was worth hundreds of dollars, and Mrs. Morris told Miss Laura that she had rather she would not wear it then, while she was a young girl. It was not suitable for her, and she knew Mrs. Drury did not expect her to do so. She wished to give her a valuable present, and this would always be worth a great deal of money.

15

Our Journey to Riverdale

Every other summer the Morris children were sent to some place in the country, so that they could have a change of air and see what country life was like. As there were so many of them, they usually went different ways for their vacations.

The summer after I came to them, Jack and Carl went to an uncle in Vermont, Miss Laura went to another in New Hampshire, and Ned and Willie went to visit a maiden aunt who lived in the White Mountains.

Mr. and Mrs. Morris stayed at home. Fairport was a lovely place in summer, and many people came there to visit and rest.

The children took some of their pets with them, and the others they left at home for their mother to take care of. She never allowed them to take a pet animal anywhere unless she knew it would be perfectly welcome. "Don't let your pets be a worry to other people," she often said to them, "or they will dislike them and you, too."

Miss Laura went away earlier than the others, for she had run down through the spring, and was pale and thin. One day early in June we set out. I say "we," for after my adventure with Jenkins, Miss Laura said that I should never be parted from her. If anyone invited her for a visit and didn't want me, she would stay at home.

The whole family went to the station to see us off. They put a chain on my collar and took me to the baggage office and got two tickets for me. One was tied to my collar, and the other Miss Laura put in her purse. Then I was put in a baggage car and chained in a corner. I heard Mr. Morris say that as we were going only a short distance, it was not worthwhile to get an express ticket for me.

There was a dreadful noise and bustle at the station. Whistles were blowing and people were rushing up and down the platform. Some men were tumbling baggage so fast into the car where I was that I was afraid some of it would fall on me.

For a few minutes Miss Laura stood by the door and looked in, but soon the men had piled up so many boxes and trunks that she could not see me. Then she went away. Mr. Morris asked one of the men to see that I did not get hurt, and I heard some money rattle. Then he went away, too.

It was the beginning of June and the weather had suddenly become very hot. We had had a long cold spring, and not being used to the heat, it seemed very hard to bear.

Before the train started, the doors of the baggage car were closed, and it became quite dark inside. The darkness, and the heat, and the close smell, and the noise as we were rushing along, made me feel sick and frightened.

I did not dare to lie down, but sat up trembling and wishing that we might soon come to Riverdale Station. But we did not get there for some time, and I was to have a great fright.

I was thinking of all the stories that I knew of animals traveling. In February, the Drurys' Newfoundland watchdog, Pluto, had arrived from New York, and he told Jim and me that he had a miserable journey.

A gentleman friend of Mr. Drury's had brought him from New York. He saw Pluto chained up in his car, and he went into his Pullman, first tipping the baggage master handsomely to look after Pluto. But Pluto said that the baggage master never once gave him a drink or anything to eat, from the time they left New York till they got to Fairport. When the train stopped there and Pluto's chain was unfastened, he sprang out onto the platform and nearly knocked Mr. Drury down. He saw some snow that had sifted through the station roof and he was so thirsty that he began to lick it up. When the snow was all gone, he jumped up and licked the frost on the windows.

Mr. Drury's friend was very angry. He found the baggage master and said to him, "What did you mean by coming into my car every few hours to tell me that the dog was fed and watered and comfortable? I shall report you."

I was not afraid of suffering like Pluto, because it was only going to take us a few hours to get to Riverdale. I found that we always went slowly before we came into a station, and one time when we began to slacken speed I thought that surely we must be at our journey's end. However, it was not Riverdale.

The car gave a kind of jump, then there was a crashing sound ahead, and we stopped.

I heard men shouting and running up and down, and I wondered what had happened. It was all dark and still in the car, and nobody came in, but the noise kept up outside, and I knew something had gone wrong with the train. Perhaps Miss Laura had got hurt. Something must have happened to her or she would come to me.

I barked and pulled at my chain till my neck was sore, but for a long, long time I was there alone. The men running about outside must have heard me. If ever I hear a man in trouble and crying for help, I go to him and see what he wants.

After such a long time that it seemed to me it must be the middle of the night, the door at the end of the car opened and a man looked in. "This is all through baggage for New York, miss," I heard him say. "They wouldn't put your dog in here."

"Yes, they did—I am sure this is the car," I heard in the voice I knew so well. "Won't you get him out, please? He must be terribly frightened."

The man stooped down and unfastened my chain, grumbling to himself because I had not been put in another car. "Some folks tumble a dog round as if he was a hunk of coal," he said, patting me kindly.

I was nearly wild with delight to get with Miss Laura again, but I had barked so much and pressed my neck so hard with my collar that my voice was all gone. I fawned on her and wagged myself about and opened and shut my mouth, but no sound came out of it.

It made Miss Laura nervous. She tried to laugh and cry at

the same time, and then she bit her lip hard and said, "Oh, Joe, don't."

"He's lost his bark, hasn't he?" said the man, looking at me curiously.

"It is a wicked thing to confine an animal in a dark, closed car," said Miss Laura, trying to see her way down the steps through her tears.

The man put out his hand and helped her. "He's not suffered much, miss," he said. "Don't you distress yourself." He lifted his cap and hurried down the platform, and Miss Laura picked her way among the bits of coal and wood scattered about the platform, and went into the waiting room of the little station.

She took me up to the filter and let some water run in her hand, and gave it to me to lap. Then she sat down, and I leaned my head against her knees, and she stroked my throat gently.

There were some people sitting about the room, and from their talk I found out what had taken place. There had been a freight train on a side track at this station, waiting for us to get by. The switchman had carelessly left the switch open, and when we came along afterward, our train, instead of running in by the platform, went crashing into the freight train. If we had been going fast, great damage might have been done. As it was, our engine was smashed so badly that it could not take us on. The passengers were frightened, and we were having a tedious time waiting for another engine to come and take us the rest of the way to Riverdale.

Some time later we were joyfully hastening to the train. It was only a few miles to Riverdale; so the conductor let me stay in the car with Miss Laura. She spread her coat out on the seat in front of her, and I sat on it and looked out of the car window as we sped along through a lovely country, all green and fresh in the June sunlight. How light and pleasant this car was—so different from the baggage car. What frightens an animal most of all things is not to see where it is going, not to know what is going to happen to it. I think that animals are very like human beings in this respect.

A lady had taken a seat beside Miss Laura, and as we went along, she, too, looked out of the window and said in a low voice:

" 'What is so rare as a day in June,

Then, if ever, come perfect days.' "

"That is very true," said Miss Laura. "How sad that the autumn must come, and the cold winter."

"No, my dear, not sad. It is but a preparation for another summer."

"Yes, I suppose it is," said Miss Laura. Then she continued a little shyly, as her companion leaned over to stroke my cropped ears, "You seem very fond of animals."

"I am, my dear. I have four horses, two cows, a tame squirrel, three dogs, and a cat."

"You should be a happy woman," said Miss Laura with a smile.

"I think I am. I must not forget my horned toad, Diego, that I got in California. I keep him in the greenhouse, and he is very happy catching flies, and holding his horny head to be scratched whenever anyone comes near."

"I don't see how anyone can be unkind to animals," said Miss Laura thoughtfully.

"Nor I, my dear child. It has always caused me intense pain to witness the torture of dumb animals. Nearly seventy years ago, when I was a little girl walking the streets of Boston, I would tremble and grow faint at the cruelty of drivers to overloaded horses. I was timid and did not dare speak to them. Very often, I ran home and flung myself in my mother's arms with a burst of tears, and asked her if nothing could be done to help the poor animals. With mistaken, motherly kindness, she tried to put the subject out of my thoughts. I was carefully guarded from seeing or hearing of any instances of cruelty.

"But the animals went on suffering just the same, and when I became a woman, I saw my cowardice. I agitated the matter among my friends, and told them that our whole dumb creation was groaning together in pain, and would continue to groan unless merciful human beings were willing to help them. I was able to assist in the formation of several societies for the prevention of cruelty to animals, and they have done good service. Good service not only to the horses and cows, but to the nobler animal, man.

"I believe that in saying to a cruel man, 'You shall not overwork, torture, mutilate, nor kill your animal, or neglect to provide it with proper food and shelter,' we are making him a little nearer the kingdom of heaven than he was before. For 'Whatsoever a man soweth, that shall he also reap.' If he sows seeds of unkindness and cruelty to man and beast, no one knows what the blackness of the harvest will be. His poor horse, quivering under a blow, is not the worst sufferer. Oh, if people would only understand that their unkind deeds will recoil upon their own heads with tenfold force—but, my child,

I am fancying that I am addressing a drawing-room meeting —and here we are at the station. Good-bye; keep your happy face and gentle ways. I hope that we may meet again soon."

She pressed Miss Laura's hand and gave me a farewell pat. The next minute we were outside on the platform, and she was smiling through the window at us.

16

Dingley Farm

M<small>Y DEAR</small> niece!" A stout, middle-aged woman with a red, lively face threw both her arms around Miss Laura. "How glad I am to see you, and this is the dog. Good Joe, I have a bone waiting for you. And here is Uncle John."

A tall, good-looking man stepped up and put out a big hand, in which my mistress's little fingers were quite swallowed up. "I am glad to see you, Laura. Well there, Beautiful Joe, how d'ye do, old boy? I've heard all about you."

It made me feel very welcome to have them both notice me, and I was so glad to be out of the train that I frisked for joy around their feet as we went to the wagon. It was a big double one with an awning over it to shelter it from the sun's rays, and the horses were drawn up in the shade of a spreading tree.

They were two powerful black horses, and as they had no blinders on, they could see us coming. Their faces lighted up and they moved their ears and pawed the ground, and whinnied when Mr. Wood went up to them. They tried to rub their heads against him, and I saw plainly that they loved him.

"Steady there, Cleve and Pacer," he said. "Now back, back up."

By this time, Mrs. Wood, Miss Laura, and I were in the wagon. Then Mr. Wood jumped in, took up the reins, and off we went. How the two black horses did spin along! I sat on the seat beside Mr. Wood, and sniffed in the delicious air and the lovely smell of flowers and grass. How glad I was to be in the country! What long races I should have in the green fields! I wished that I had another dog to run with me, and wondered very much whether Mr. Wood kept one. I knew I should soon find out, for whenever Miss Laura went to a place she wanted to know what animals were about.

We drove a little more than a mile along a country road where there were scattered houses. Miss Laura answered questions about her family, and asked questions about Mr. Harry, who was away at college and hadn't got home. I don't think I have said before that Mr. Harry was Mrs. Wood's son. She was a widow with one son when she married Mr. Wood, so that Mr. Harry, though the Morrises called him cousin, was not really their cousin.

I was very glad to hear them say that he was coming home soon, for I had never forgotten that but for him I should not have had my pleasant home.

By and by I heard Miss Laura say, "Uncle John, do you have a dog?"

"Yes, Laura," he said. "I have one today, but I shan't have one tomorrow."

"Oh, Uncle, what do you mean?" she asked.

"Well, Laura," he replied, "you know animals are pretty much like people. There are some good ones and some bad ones. Now, this dog is a snarling, cross-grained, cantankerous beast, and when I heard Joe was coming, I said, 'Now we'll have a good dog about the place, and here's an end to the bad one.' So I tied Bruno up, and tomorrow I shall shoot him, before he bites someone."

"Uncle," said Miss Laura, "people don't always die when they are bitten by dogs, do they?"

"No, certainly not," replied Mr. Wood. "At the same time dogs have no business to bite, and I don't recommend anyone to get bitten. Hydrophobia is not to be laughed at, though I believe that a careful examination of the records of Boston show that only two people died of it in the space of thirty-two years. But one can't be too careful. After all," he went on, "dogs are like all other animals. They're liable to sickness, and they've got to be watched. I think my horses would go mad if I starved them, or overfed them, or overworked them, or let them stand in laziness, or kept them dirty, or didn't give them water enough. They'd get some disease, anyway. If a person owns an animal, let him take care of it, and it's all right. If it shows signs of sickness, shut it up and watch it. If the sickness is incurable, put it out of its misery. Another way of preventing hydrophobia is not to let ownerless, vicious dogs roam the streets. If you can't do that, have plenty of water where they can get it. A dog that has plenty of water will never go mad.

"This dog of mine has not one single thing the matter with

him but pure ugliness. Yet, if I let him loose, and he ran through the village with his tongue out, I'll warrant you there'd be a cry of 'mad dog!' And if he by chance bit some fine lady or gentleman, they would hurry across to France to get Pasteur to cure them, whether they had hydrophobia or not.

"However, I'm going to kill him. I've no use for bad dogs. Have plenty of animals, I say, and treat them kindly, but if there's a vicious one among them, put it out of the way, for it is a constant danger to man and beast. It's queer how ugly some people are about their dogs. They'll keep them no matter how they worry other people, and even when they're snatching the bread out of their neighbors' mouths. But I say that is not the fault of the four-legged dog. A human dog is the worst of all.

"There's a band of sheep-killing dogs here in Riverdale that their owners can't, or won't, keep out of mischief. Meeklooking fellows some of them are. The owners go to bed at night, and the dogs pretend to go, too. But when the house is quiet and the family asleep, off goes Rover or Fido to worry poor, weak creatures that can't defend themselves." Mr. Wood shook his head. "Once a dog has the taste for sheep's blood in him, you can't get it out."

"Mr. Windham cured his dog," said Mrs. Wood.

Mr. Wood burst into a hearty laugh. "So he did, so he did. I must tell Laura about that. Windham is a neighbor of ours, and last summer I kept telling him that Dash, his collie, was worrying my Shropshires. He wouldn't believe me, but I knew I was right, and one night when Harry was home, he lay in wait for the dog and lassoed him. I tied him up and sent for Windham. You should have seen his face, and the dog's face.

He said two words, 'You scoundrel!' The dog cowered at his feet as if he had been shot.

"Then Windham asked me where my sheep were. I told him in the pasture. He asked me if I still had my old ram, Bolton. I said yes, and then he wanted eight or ten feet of rope. I gave it to him and wondered what on earth he was going to do with it. He tied one end of it to Dash's collar and, holding the other in his hand, set out for the pasture. He asked us to go with him, and when we got there, he asked Harry to catch Bolton. There wasn't any need to catch him— he'd come to us like a dog. Harry whistled, and when Bolton came up, Windham fastened the rope's end to his horns and let him go. The ram was frightened and ran, dragging the dog with him.

"We let them out of the pasture into an open field, and for a few minutes there was such a racing and chasing over that field as I never saw before. Harry leaned up against the bars and laughed till the tears rolled down his cheeks. Then Bolton got mad, and began to make battle with the dog, pitching into him with his horns. We soon stopped that, for the spirit had all gone out of Dash. Windham unfastened the rope and told him to get home, and if ever I saw a dog run, that one did. Mrs. Windham set great store by him, and her husband didn't want to kill him. But he said Dash had got to give up worrying sheep if he wanted to live. That cured him. He's never worried a sheep from that day to this, and if you offer him a bit of sheep's wool now, he tucks his tail between his legs and runs for home."

We had come to a turn in the road where the ground sloped gently upward. We turned in at the gate and drove between rows of trees up to a long, low, red house with a veranda all round it. There was a wide lawn in front, and away on our right were the farm buildings. They, too, were painted red, and there were some trees by them that Mr. Wood called his windbreak, because they kept the snow from drifting in the wintertime.

I thought it was a beautiful place. Miss Laura had been here before, but not for some years, so she, too, was looking about quite eagerly.

"Welcome to Dingley Farm, Joe," said Mrs. Wood with her jolly laugh as she watched me jump from the carriage seat to the ground. "Come in, and I'll introduce you to our pussy."

"Aunt Hattie, why is the farm called Dingley Farm?" said Miss Laura as we went into the house. "It ought to be Wood Farm."

"Dingley is made out of 'dingle,' Laura. You know that pretty hollow back of the pasture? It is what they call a 'dingle.' So this farm was called Dingle Farm till the people around about got to saying 'Dingley' instead. I suppose they found it easier. Why, here is Lolo coming in to see Joe."

Walking along the wide hall that ran through the house was a large tortoiseshell cat. She had a prettily marked face, and she was waving her large tail like a flag, and mewing kindly to greet her mistress. But when she saw me, what a face she made! She flew onto the hall table and, putting up her back till it almost lifted her feet from the ground, began to spit at me and bristle with rage.

"Poor Lolo," said Mrs. Wood, going up to her. "Joe is a good dog, and not like Bruno. He won't hurt you."

I wagged myself about a little and looked kindly at her, but she did nothing but say bad words to me. It was weeks and weeks before I made friends with that cat. She was a young thing and had known only one dog, and he was a bad one. So she supposed all dogs were like him.

There were a number of rooms opening off the hall, and one of them was the dining room where they had tea. I lay on a rug outside the door and watched them. There was a small table spread with a white cloth, and it had pretty dishes and glassware on it, and a good many different kinds of things to eat. A little French girl called Adele kept coming and going from the kitchen to give them hot cakes and fried eggs and hot coffee. As soon as they finished their tea, Mrs. Wood gave me one of the best meals I ever had in my life.

17

Mr. Wood and His Horses

THE MORNING after we arrived in Riverdale, I was up very early and walking around the house. I slept in the woodshed and could run outdoors whenever I liked.

The woodshed was at the back of the house, and near it was the tool shed. Then there was a carriage house, and a plank walk leading to the barnyard.

I ran up this walk and looked into the first building I came to. It was the horse stable. There were several horses there, some with their heads toward me, and some with their tails. I saw that, instead of being tied up, they had gates outside their stalls, and they could stand in any way they liked.

There was a man moving about at the other end of the stable, and long before he saw me, I knew that it was Mr.

Wood. What a nice clean stable he had! There were a number of little gratings in the wall to let in the fresh air, and they were so placed that drafts could not blow on the horses. Mr. Wood was going from one horse to another, giving them hay, and talking to them in a cheerful voice.

At last he spied me and cried out, "The top of the morning to you, Joe! You are up early. Don't come too near the horses, good dog," as I walked in beside him. "They might think you are another Bruno, and give you a sly bite or kick. I should have shot him long ago. 'Tis hard to make a good dog suffer for a bad one, but that's the way of the world. Well, old fellow, what do you think of my horse stable? Pretty fair, isn't it?" And Mr. Wood went on talking to me as he fed and groomed his horses, till I soon found out that his chief pride was in them.

I like to have human beings to talk to me. Mr. Morris often reads his sermons to me, and Miss Laura tells me secrets that I don't think she would tell to anyone else.

I watched Mr. Wood carefully, while he groomed a huge, gray cart horse that he called Dutchman. He took a brush in his right hand, and a currycomb in his left, and he curried and brushed every part of the horse's skin, and afterward wiped him with a cloth. "A good grooming is equal to two quarts of oats, Joe," he said to me.

Then he stooped down and examined the horse's hoofs. "Your shoes are too heavy, Dutchman," he said. "But that pig-headed blacksmith thinks he knows more about horses than I do. 'Don't cut the sole nor the frog,' I say to him. 'Don't pare the hoof so much, and don't rasp it; and fit your shoes to the foot, and not the foot to the shoe.' And he looks at me as if to say, 'Mind your own business.' We'll not go to him again.

I got you to work for me, not to wear out your strength in lifting his heavy shoes."

Mr. Wood stopped talking for a few minutes and whistled a tune. Then he began again. "I've made a study of horses, Joe. Over forty years I've studied them, and it's my opinion that the average horse knows more than the average man that drives him. Think of the stupid fools that are goading patient horses about, beating them and misunderstanding them, and thinking they are only clods of earth with a little life in them! I'd like to take their horses out of the shafts and harness them in, and I'd trot them off at a pace and slash them and jerk them till I guess they'd come out with a little less patience than the animal does.

"Look at this Dutchman—see the size of him! You'd think he hadn't any more nerves than a chunk of granite. Yet he's got a skin as sensitive as a girl's. See how he quivers if I run the currycomb too harshly over him. The idiot I got him from didn't know what was the matter with him. He'd bought him for a reliable horse, and there he was, kicking and stamping whenever the boy went near him. 'Your boy's got too heavy a hand, Deacon Jones,' said I, when he described the horse's actions to me. 'You may depend upon it, a four-legged creature, unlike a two-legged one, has a reason for everything he does.'

" 'But he's only a draft horse,' said Deacon Jones. 'Draft horse or no draft horse,' said I, 'you're describing a horse with a tender skin to me, and I don't care if he's as big as an elephant.' Well, the old man grumbled and said he didn't want any thoroughbred airs in his stable. So I bought you, didn't I, Dutchman?" And Mr. Wood stroked him kindly and went to the next stall.

In each stall was a small tank of water with a sliding cover, and I found out afterward that these covers were put on when a horse came in too heated to have a drink. At any other time he could drink all he liked. Mr. Wood believed in having plenty of pure water for all his animals, and they all had their own place to get a drink.

Even I had a little bowl of water in the woodshed, though I could easily have run up to the barnyard when I wanted a drink. As soon as I came, Mrs. Wood asked Adele to keep it there for me and when I looked up gratefully at her, she said, "Every animal should have its own feeding place and sleeping place, Joe. That is only fair."

The next horses Mr. Wood groomed were the black ones, Cleve and Pacer. Pacer had something wrong with his mouth and Mr. Wood turned back his lips and examined it carefully. This he was able to do, for there were large windows in the stable and it was as light as Mr. Wood's house was.

"No dark corners here, eh, Joe!" said Mr. Wood as he came out of the stall and passed me to get a bottle from a shelf. "When this stable was built, I said no dirt holes for careless men here. I want the sun to shine in the corners, and I don't want my horses to smell bad smells, for they hate them, and I don't want them starting when they go into the light of day, just because they've been kept in a black hole of a stable. And I've never had a sick horse yet."

He poured something from a bottle into a saucer and went back to Pacer with it. I followed him and stood outside. Mr. Wood seemed to be washing a sore in the horse's mouth. Pacer winced a little, and Mr. Wood said, "Steady, steady, my beauty. 'Twill soon be over."

The horse fixed his intelligent eyes on his master and

looked as if he knew Mr. Wood was trying to do him good.

"Just look at these lips, Joe," said Mr. Wood. "Delicate and fine like our own, and yet there are brutes that will jerk them as if they were made of iron. I wish the Lord would give horses voices for just one week. I tell you they'd scare some of us. Now, Pacer, that's over. I'm not going to dose you much, for I don't believe in it. If a horse has got a serious trouble, get a good horse doctor, say I. If it's a simple thing, try a simple remedy. There's been many a good horse drugged and dosed to death. Well, Scamp, my beauty, how are you this morning?"

In the stall next to Pacer was a small, jet-black mare with a lean head, slender legs, and a curious, restless manner. She was a regular greyhound of a horse, no spare flesh, yet wiry and able to do a great deal of work. She was a wicked-looking little thing; so I thought I had better keep at a safe distance from her heels.

Mr. Wood petted her a great deal and I saw that she was his favorite. "Saucebox!" he exclaimed when she pretended to bite him. "You know if you bite me, I'll bite back again. I think I've conquered you," he said proudly as he stroked her glossy neck. "But what a dance you led me! Do you remember how I bought you for a mere song, because you had a bad habit of turning around like a flash in front of anything that frightened you, and bolting off the other way? And how did I cure you, my beauty? Beat you and make you stubborn? Not I. I let you go round and round. I turned you and twisted you, the oftener the better for me, till at last I got it into your pretty head that turning and twisting was addling your brains, and you had better let me be your master.

"You've minded me from that day, haven't you? Horse, or man, or dog isn't much good till he learns to obey. I've thrown you down, and I'll do it again if you bite me, so take care."

Scamp tossed her pretty head and took little pieces of Mr. Wood's shirt sleeve in her mouth, keeping her cunning brown eye on him as if to see how far she could go. But she did not bite him. When he left her she whinnied shrilly, and he had to go back and caress her.

After Mr. Wood finished his work he went and stood in the doorway. There were six horses altogether: Dutchman, Cleve, Pacer, Scamp, a bay mare called Ruby, and a young horse belonging to Mr. Harry, whose name was Fleetfoot.

"A fine-looking lot of horses, aren't they?" said Mr. Wood, looking down at me. "Not a thoroughbred there, but worth as much to me as if each had a pedigree as long as this plank walk. There's a lot of humbug about this pedigree business in horses. Mine have their manes and tails, anyway, and the proper use of their eyes, which is more liberty than some thoroughbreds get.

"I'd like to see the man that would persuade me to put blinders or checkreins or any other instrument of torture on my horses. Don't the simpletons know that blinders are the cause of—well, I wouldn't like to say how many of our accidents, Joe, for fear you'd think me extravagant. And the checkrein drags up a horse's head out of its fine natural curve and presses sinews, bones, and joints together, till the horse is well-nigh mad. Ah, Joe, this is a cruel world for man or beast. You're a standing token of that, with your missing ears and tail. And now I've got to go and be cruel and shoot Bruno. I hate to do it."

"Let me look at Bruno, Uncle John," said a soft voice from behind. It was my dear Miss Laura. Mr. Wood looked surprised. Then he shrugged.

"I warn you, Bruno is a vicious dog," said Mr. Wood as he led us to the large brown dog chained behind one of the sheds. "Be careful," he admonished as Miss Laura knelt beside the dog. He must have seen the love for all animals that showed in her eyes. He made no move to snap at her.

Slowly, ever so slowly, her hand crept near him; then she was stroking his coat; then she was running her fingers through his fur, touching his skin. The big dog flinched, but he kept looking steadily and somehow trustfully up into her kind face. Suddenly her fingers stopped. Bruno gave a howl of pain, a savage howl. Hastily Miss Laura got up.

"Have you looked over his coat recently, Uncle John?" she asked.

"Not since three weeks ago when he almost bit me."

Miss Laura looked down at the dog at her feet. "That must have been about the time when that wood tick started burrowing into his flesh. He has a nasty sore there now."

Mr. Wood shook his head. He scratched his nose. Then he said, "And to think I was about to kill that poor creature! I, who pride myself on my care and kindness to animals. You have proved to me, Miss Laura, something I have known all along yet needed to be reminded of, the wisdom of the old saying, 'One can never be too careful.' I shall tie up Bruno and remove the tick this morning."

The wood tick was removed later that morning, and for the rest of my stay there Bruno was a good-natured, well-behaved dog, and we became good friends.

But in the meantime we heard the breakfast bell and hurried back to the house. Miss Laura had such a good appetite for her breakfast that her aunt said the country had done her good already.

18

Mrs. Wood's Poultry

AFTER BREAKFAST, Mrs. Wood put on a large apron and, going into the kitchen, said, "Have you any scraps for the hens, Adele? Be sure and not give me anything that is salty."

The French girl gave her a dish of food, and then Mrs. Wood asked Miss Laura to go and see her chickens. Away we went to the poultry house.

"Here we are at the hen house," said Mrs. Wood, stopping before a small building, "or, rather, at one of the hen houses."

"Don't you keep all your hens in the same house?" asked Miss Laura.

"Only in the wintertime," said Mrs. Wood. "I divide my flock in the spring. Part of them stay here and part go to the orchard to live in little movable houses that we put about in different places. I feed each flock morning and evening at their own little house. They know they'll get no food even if they come to my house, so they stay at home. And they know they'll get no food between times, so all day long they pick and scratch in the orchard, and destroy so many bugs and insects that it more than pays for the trouble of keeping them there."

"Doesn't this flock want to mix with the other?" asked Miss Laura as she stepped into the little wooden house.

"No, they seem to understand. I keep my eye on them for a while at first, and they soon find out that they're not to fly either over the garden fence or the orchard fence. They roam over the farm and pick up what they can get. There's a good deal of sense in hens, if one manages them properly. I love them because they are such good mothers."

We were in the little wooden house by this time, and I looked around it with surprise. The walls were white and clean, and so were the little ladders that led up to different kinds of roosts, where the fowls sat at night. Some roosts were thin and round, and some were broad and flat. Mrs. Wood said that the broad ones were for heavy fowls called the Brahmas. Every part of the little house was almost as light and sunny as it was out of doors, on account of several large windows.

Miss Laura spoke of it. "Why, Auntie, I never saw such a light hen house."

"Yes," smiled Mrs. Wood. "There's not another hen house in New Hampshire with such big windows. Whenever I look at them, I think of my mother's hens, and wish that they could have a place like this. They would have thought themselves in a hen's paradise. When I was a little girl, we didn't know that hens loved light and heat, and all winter they used to sit in a dark hen coop, and the cold was so bad that their combs would freeze. We never thought about it. If we'd had any sense, we might have watched them on a fine day go and sit on the compost heap and sun themselves, and then have concluded that if they liked light and heat outside, they'd like it inside. Poor biddies, they were so cold that they wouldn't lay us any eggs in winter."

"You take a great interest in your poultry, don't you, Auntie?" said Miss Laura.

"Yes, indeed, and well I may. I'll show you my brown leghorn, Jenny, that lays eggs enough in a year to pay for the newspapers I take to keep myself posted on poultry matters. I buy all my own clothes with my hen money, and lately I've started a bank account, for I want to save up enough to start a few stands of bees. Even if I didn't want to be kind to my hens, it would pay me to be so for the sake of the profit they yield. I always say to anyone that thinks of raising poultry, 'If you are going into the business to make money, it pays to take care of them.' "

"There's one thing I notice," said Miss Laura. "That is that your drinking fountains must be a great deal better than the shallow pans that I have seen some people give their hens water in."

"Unsanitary things they are," said Mrs. Wood. "I wouldn't use one of them. I don't think there is anything worse for hens than impure drinking water. My hens must have as clean water as I drink myself, and in winter I heat it for them. If it's poured boiling into the fountains in the morning, it keeps warm till night. Speaking of shallow drinking dishes, I wouldn't use them, even before I heard of a drinking fountain. John made me something that we read about. He used to take a keg and bore a little hole in the side, about an inch from the top, then fill it with water, and cover it with a pan a little larger around than the keg. Then he turned the keg upside down, without taking away the pan. The water ran into the pan only as far as the hole in the keg, and it had to be used before more would flow in.

"Now let us go and see my beautiful bronze turkeys. They don't need any houses, for they roost in the trees the year round."

We found the flock of turkeys, and Miss Laura admired their changeable colors very much. Some of them were very large, and I did not like them, for the gobblers ran at me and made a dreadful noise in their throats.

Every place Mrs. Wood showed us was as clean as possible. "No one can be successful in raising poultry in large numbers," she said, "unless he keeps their quarters clean and comfortable."

As yet we had seen no hens, except a few on the nests, and Miss Laura asked, "Where are all the hens? I should like to see them."

"They are coming," said Mrs. Wood. "It is just their breakfast time, and they are as punctual as clockwork. They go off early in the morning to scratch about a little for themselves first."

As she spoke she stepped off the plank walk, and looked off toward the fields.

Miss Laura burst out laughing. Away beyond the barns the hens were coming. Seeing Mrs. Wood standing there, they thought they were late, and they began to run and fly, jumping over each other's backs and stretching out their necks in a state of great excitement. Some of their legs seemed sticking out straight behind. It was very funny to see them.

They were a fine-looking lot of poultry, mostly white, with glossy feathers and bright eyes.

"They think I've changed their breakfast time, and tomorrow they'll come a good bit earlier. And yet some people say hens have no sense," said Mrs. Wood as they greedily ate the food that she scattered to them.

19

A Band of Mercy

A FEW EVENINGS after we came to Dingley Farm, Mrs. Wood and Miss Laura were sitting on the veranda, and I was lying at their feet.

"Auntie," said Miss Laura, "what do those letters mean on that silver pin you are wearing?"

Mrs. Wood touched the little star pin. "This," she said, "means that I am a member of a Band of Mercy. Do you know what a Band of Mercy is?"

"No," said Miss Laura.

"How strange! I should think that you would have several in Fairport. A crippled boy, the son of a Boston artist, started this one. It has done a great deal of good. There is a meeting tomorrow, and I will take you to it if you would like to go."

The next afternoon, after all the work was done, they got ready to go to the village.

"May Joe go?" asked Miss Laura.

"Certainly," said Mrs. Wood. "He is such a good dog that he won't be any trouble. Perhaps in a few weeks, when Bruno's wound is healed and he is well in mind and body, he can go, too."

I was very glad to hear this, and trotted along by them down the lane to the road. The lane was a very cool and pleasant place. There were tall trees growing on each side, and under them in the grass pretty wild flowers were peeping out to look at us as we went by.

Mrs. Wood and Miss Laura talked all the way about the Band of Mercy. Miss Laura was much interested and said that she would like to start one in Fairport.

"It is a very simple thing," said Mrs. Wood. "All you have to do is to write the pledge at the top of a piece of paper: 'I will try to be kind to all harmless living creatures, and try to protect them from cruel usage.' Then get thirty people to sign it. That makes a band.

"A Band of Mercy is a splendid thing. There's the greatest difference in Riverdale since this one was started. A few years ago, when a man beat or raced his horse and anyone interfered, he said: 'This horse is mine; I'll do what I like with him.' Most people thought he was right, but now they're all for the poor horse, and there isn't a man anywhere around who would dare to abuse any animal.

"All the children belong. They're doing a grand work, and I say it's a good thing for them. A child is such a tender thing. You can bend him any way you like. Many school teachers say that there is nothing better than to give them lessons on

kindness to animals. Children who are taught to love and protect dumb creatures will be kind to their fellow men when
they grow up."

I was very much pleased with this talk between Mrs. Wood
and Miss Laura, and kept close to them so that I would not
miss a word.

As we went along, houses began to appear here and there,
set back from the road among the trees. Soon they got quite
close together, and I saw some shops.

This was the village of Riverdale, and nearly all the buildings were along this winding street. The river was away back
of the village. We had already driven there several times.

We passed the school on our way. It was a square white
building, standing in the middle of a large yard. Boys and
girls, with their arms full of books, were hurrying down the
steps and coming into the street. Two quite big boys came
behind us, and Mrs. Wood turned around and spoke to them,
and asked if they were going to the meeting of the Band of
Mercy.

"Oh, yes, ma'am," said the younger one. "I've got a recitation, don't you remember?"

"Yes, yes, excuse me for forgetting," said Mrs. Wood with
a jolly laugh. "And here are Dolly and Jennie and Martha,"
she went on, as some little girls came running out of a house
that we were passing.

The little girls joined us and looked so hard at my head
and stump of a tail, and my fine collar, that I felt shy and
walked with my head against Miss Laura's dress. She stooped
down and patted me, and then I felt as if I didn't care how
much they stared.

Mrs. Wood paused in front of a building on the main street.

A great many boys and girls were going in, and we went with them. We found ourselves in a large room with a platform at one end of it. There were some chairs on this platform and a small table.

A boy stood by this table with his hand on a bell. Presently he rang it, and then everyone kept still. Mrs. Wood whispered to Miss Laura that this boy was the president of the band, and the young man with the pale face and curly hair who sat in front of him was Mr. Maxwell, the artist's son, who had formed this Band of Mercy.

The lad who presided had a ringing, pleasant voice. He said they would begin their meeting by singing a hymn. There was an organ near the platform, and a young girl played on it, while all the other boys and girls stood up and sang very sweetly and clearly.

After they had sung the hymn, the president asked for the report of their last meeting.

A little girl, blushing and hanging her head, came forward and read what was written on a paper that she held in her hand.

The president made some remarks after she had finished, and then everyone had to vote. After the voting was over, the president called upon John Turner to give a recitation. This was the boy whom we saw on the way there. He walked up to the platform, made a bow, and said that he had learned two stories for his recitation out of the paper, "Dumb Animals." One story was about a horse, and the other was about a dog, and he thought that they were two of the best animal stories on record. He would tell the horse story first.

"A man in Missouri had to go to Nebraska to see about some land. He went on horseback, on a horse that he had trained himself, and that came at his whistle like a dog. On getting into Nebraska, he came to a place where there were two roads. One went by a river, and the other went over the hill.

"The man saw that the traffic went over the hill, but thought he'd take the river road. He didn't know that there was quicksand across it, and that people couldn't use it in spring and summer. There used to be a signboard to tell strangers about it, but it had been taken away. The man got off his horse to let him graze, and walked along till he got so far ahead of the horse that he had to sit down and wait for him. Suddenly he found he was on quicksand. His feet had sunk in the sand, and he could not get them out again.

"He threw himself down, and whistled for his horse, and shouted for help, but no one came. He could hear some young people singing out on the river, but they could not hear him. The terrible sand drew him in almost to his shoulders, and he thought he was lost. At that moment the horse came running up, and stood by his master. The man was too low down to get hold of the saddle or bridle, so he took hold of the horse's tail and told him to go. The horse gave an awful pull, and finally he landed his master on safe ground."

Everybody clapped his hands and stamped his feet when this story was finished, and called out, "The dog story—the dog story!"

The boy bowed and smiled, and began again. "You all know what a 'roundup' of cattle is, so I need not explain. Once a man down south was going to have one, and he and his boys and friends were talking it over. There was an ugly black steer in the herd, and they were wondering whether their old yellow dog would be able to manage him.

"The dog's name was Tige, and he lay and listened wisely to their talk. The next day there was a scene of great confusion. The steer raged and tore about, and would allow no one to come within whip touch of him. Tige, who had always been brave, skulked about for a while, and then, as if he had got up a little spirit, he made a quick run at the steer.

"The steer sighted him, gave a bellow, and, lowering his horns, ran at him. Tige turned tail, and the young men that owned him were frantic. They'd been praising him, and thought they were going to be proved wrong. Their father called out, 'Don't shoot Tige, till you see where he's running to.' The dog ran right to the cattle pen. The steer was so enraged that he never noticed where he was going, and dashed in after him.

"Tige leaped the wall and came back to the gate, barking and yelping for the men to come and shut the steer in. They shut the gate and petted Tige, and bought him a collar with a silver plate."

The boy was loudly cheered and went to his seat. The president said he would like to have remarks made about these two stories.

Several children put up their hands, and he asked each one to speak in turn. One said that if that man's horse had had a docked tail, his master wouldn't have been able to reach it, and would have perished. Another said that if the man hadn't treated his horse kindly, he never would have come at his whistle, and stood over him to see what he could do to help him. A third child said that the people on the river weren't as quick to hear the voice of the man in trouble as the horse was.

When this talk was over the president called for more animal stories.

20

Stories About Animals

THREE OR four boys jumped up, but the president said they would take one at a time. The first story was this: A Riverdale boy was walking along the bank of a canal in Hoytville. He saw a boy driving two horses, which were towing a canalboat. The first horse was slow, and the boy got angry and struck him several times over the head with his whip. The Riverdale boy shouted across to him, begging him not to be so cruel. But the other boy paid no attention.

Suddenly the horse turned, seized his tormentor by the shoulder, and pushed him into the canal. The water was not deep, and the boy, after floundering about for a few seconds, came out dripping and sat down on the tow path and looked at the

horse with such a comical expression that the Riverdale boy had to stuff his handkerchief in his mouth to keep from laughing.

"It is to be hoped that he learned a lesson," said the president, "and will be kinder to his horse in the future. Now, Bernard Howe, your story."

Bernard told his story and Miss Laura listened eagerly, for it was about Fairport.

The boy said that when his grandfather was young, he lived in Fairport, Maine. On a certain day he stood in the market square to see their first stagecoach put together. It had come from Boston in pieces, for there was no one in Fairport that could make one. The coach went away up into the country one day and came back the next.

For a long time no one understood driving the horses properly, and they came in day after day with blood streaming

from them. The whiffletree would swing around and hit them, and when their collars were taken off, their necks would be raw and bloody. After some time, the men learned how to drive a coach, and the horses did not suffer so much.

When this boy took his seat, a young girl read some verses that she had clipped from a newspaper:

"Don't kill the toads, the ugly toads,
    That hop around your door;
Each meal the little toad doth eat
    A hundred bugs or more.

"He sits around with aspect meek,
    Until the bug hath neared,
Then shoots he forth his little tongue
    Like lightning double-geared.

"And then he soberly doth wink,
 And shut his ugly mug,
And patiently doth wait until
 There comes another bug."

Then the president said that he would like to know what
the members had been doing for animals during the past
fortnight.

One girl had kept her brother from shooting two owls that
came about their barnyard. She told him that the owls would
destroy the rats and mice that bothered him in the barn, but
if he hunted the birds, they would leave the barnyard and go
to the woods.

A little girl had stopped a man in the street who was carrying a pair of fowls with their heads down, and asked him if
he would kindly reverse their position. The man told her that
fowls didn't mind, and she pursed up her small mouth and
showed the band how she said to him, "I would prefer the
opinion of the hens." Then she said he had laughed at her,
and said, "Certainly, little lady," and had gone off carrying
them as she wanted him to. She had also reasoned with different boys outside the village who were throwing stones at birds
and frogs, and sticking butterflies, and had invited them to
come to the meetings of the Band of Mercy.

This child seemed to have done more than anyone else for
dumb animals. She had taken around a petition to the village
boys, asking them not to search for birds' eggs, and she had
even gone into her father's stable and asked him to hold her
up, so that she could look into the horses' mouths to see if
their teeth wanted filing or were decayed. When her father
laughed at her, she told him that horses often suffer terrible

pain from their teeth, and that sometimes a runaway is caused by a metal bit striking against the exposed nerve in the tooth of a horse that had become almost frantic with pain.

She was a very gentle little girl, and I think by the way she spoke that her father loved her dearly, for she told how much trouble he had taken to make some tiny houses for her that she wanted for the wrens that came about their farm. She told him that those little birds are so good at catching insects that they ought to give all their time to it, and not have any worry about making houses. Her father made their homes very small, so that the English sparrows could not get in and crowd them out.

A boy said that he had painted in large letters on the fences around his father's farm: *Spare the toads, don't kill the birds. Every bird killed is a loss to the country.*

"That reminds me," said the president, "to ask the girls what they have done about the millinery business."

"I have told my mother," said a tall, serious-faced girl, "that I think it is wrong to wear bird feathers, and she has promised to give up wearing any of them."

Mrs. Wood asked permission to say a few words just here, and the president said, "Certainly, we are always glad to hear from you."

She went up on the platform, and faced the roomful of children.

"Dear boys and girls," she began, "I have had some papers sent me from Boston, giving some facts about the killing of our birds, and I want to state a few of them to you. You all know that nearly every tree and plant swarms with insect life, and the plants couldn't grow if the birds didn't eat the insects that would devour their foliage. All day long, the little beaks of the birds are busy. The dear little rosebreasted grosbeak carefully examines the potato plants and picks off the beetles. The martins destroy weevils. The quail and grouse family eat the chinch bug. The woodpeckers dig the worms from the trees. Many other birds eat the flies and gnats and mosquitoes that torment us. No flying or crawling creature escapes their sharp little eyes. A great Frenchman says that if it weren't for the birds, human beings would soon perish from the face of the earth.

"They are doing all this for us, and how are we rewarding them? All over America they are hunted and killed. Five million birds must be caught every year for American women to wear in their hats and bonnets. Just think of it, girls. Isn't it dreadful? Five million innocent, hard-working, beautiful birds killed, that thoughtless girls and women may ornament themselves with their little dead bodies. One million bobolinks have been killed in one month near Philadelphia. Seventy songbirds were sent from one Long Island village to New York milliners.

"In Florida, cruel men shoot the mother birds on the nests while they are rearing their young, because their plumage is prettiest at that time. The little ones cry pitifully, and starve to death. Every bird of the rarer kinds that is killed, such as hummingbirds, orioles, and kingfishers, means the death of several others—that is, the young which starve to death, the wounded that fly away to die, and those whose plumage is so torn that it is not fit to put in a fine lady's bonnet. In some cases where birds have gay wings, and the hunters do not wish the rest of the body, they tear off the beautiful wings and throw the poor birds away to die.

"I am sorry to tell you such painful things, but I think you

ought to know them. You will soon be men and women. Do
what you can to stop this horrid trade. Our beautiful birds
are being taken from us, and the insect pests are increasing.
The State of Massachusetts has lost over one hundred thou-
sand dollars because it did not protect its birds. The gypsy
moth stripped the trees near Boston, and the State had to pay
out all this money, and even then could not get rid of the
moths. The birds could have done it better than the State, but
they were all gone. My last words to you are, 'Protect the
birds.' "

Mrs. Wood went to her seat, and though the boys and girls
had listened very attentively, none of them cheered her. Their
faces looked sad, and they kept very quiet for a few minutes.
I saw one or two little girls wiping their eyes. I think they felt
sorry for the birds.

"Has any boy done anything about blinders and check-
reins?" asked the president, after a time.

A brown-faced boy stood up. "I had a picnic last Monday,"
he said. "Father let me cut all the blinders off our headstalls
with my penknife."

"How did you get him to consent to that?" asked the president.

"I told him," said the boy, "that I couldn't get to sleep for
thinking of him. You know he drives a good deal late at night.
I told him that every dark night he came from Sudbury I
thought of the deep ditch alongside the road, and wished his
horses hadn't blinders on. On some nights he comes from the
Junction and has to drive along the river bank where the water
has washed away the earth till the wheels of the wagon are
within a foot or two of the edge. So I wished again that his
horses could see each side of them, for I knew they'd have

sense enough to keep out of danger if they could see it.

"Father said that might be very true, and yet his horses had been broken in with blinders, and didn't I think they would be inclined to shy if he took them off? And wouldn't they be frightened to look around and see the wagon wheels so near? I told him that for every accident that happened to a horse without blinders, several happened to a horse with them.

"Then I gave him Mr. Wood's opinion—Mr. Wood out at Dingley Farm. He says that the worst thing against blinders is that a frightened horse never knows when he has passed the thing that scared him. He always thinks it is beside him. The blinders are there and he can't see that he has passed it, and he can't turn his head to have a good look at it. So often he goes tearing madly on, and sometimes lives are lost all on account of a little bit of leather fastened over a beautiful eye that ought to look out full and free at the world.

"That finished Father. He said he'd take off his blinders, and if he had an accident, he'd send the bill for damages to Mr. Wood. But we've had no accident. The horses did act rather queerly at first, and started a little, but they soon got over it, and now they go as steady without blinders as they did with them."

The boy sat down, and the president said, "I think it is time that the whole nation threw off this foolishness of half covering their horses' eyes. Just put your hands up to your eyes, members of the band. Half cover them, and see how shut in you feel, and how curious you will be to know what is going on beside you. Suppose a girl saw a mouse with her eyes half covered, wouldn't she run?"

Everybody laughed, and the president asked someone to

tell him who invented blinders.

"An English nobleman," shouted a boy, "who had a wall-eyed horse! He wanted to cover up the defect, and I think it is a great shame that all the American horses have to suffer because that English one had an ugly eye."

"So do I," said the president. "Let's all give three groans for blinders."

All the children in the room made three dreadful noises away down in their throats. Then they had another good laugh, and the president became sober again. "Seven more minutes," he said. "This meeting must let out at five o'clock sharp."

A tall girl in the back of the room rose and said, "My little cousin has a story she would like to tell the band."

"Very well," said the president. "Bring her right along."

The big girl came forward, leading a tiny child that she placed in front of the boys and girls. The child stared up into her cousin's face, turning and twisting her white pinafore through her fingers. Every time the big girl took her pinafore away from her, she picked it up again.

"Begin, Nannie," said the big girl kindly.

"Well, Cousin Eleanor," said the child, "you know Tiger, our big dog. He used to be a bad dog, and when Dr. Fairchild drove up to the house he jumped up and bit at him. Dr. Fairchild started speaking kindly to him and throwing him bits of meat, and now when he comes, Tiger follows behind and wags his tail."

Eleanor smiled down at her little cousin. "Well done, Nannie," she said. While the other children clapped their hands, she led the little girl back to their seats.

There was one more story, about a brave Newfoundland

dog that saved eight lives by swimming out to a wrecked sailing vessel and getting a rope by which the men came ashore. Then a lad got up whom they all greeted with cheers and cries of, "The Poet! The Poet!" I didn't know what they meant till Mrs. Wood whispered to Miss Laura that he was a boy who made rhymes, and the children had rather hear him speak than anyone else in the room.

He had a snub nose and freckles, and I think he was the plainest boy there, but that didn't matter if the other children loved him. He sauntered up to the front, with his hands behind his back and a very grand manner.

"The beautiful poetry recited here today," he drawled, "put some verses in my mind that I never had till I came here today." Everyone present cheered wildly, and he began in a singsong voice:

> "I am a Band of Mercy boy,
>   I would not hurt a fly,
> I always speak to dogs and cats,
>   When'er I pass them by.
>
> "I always let the birdies sing,
>   I never throw a stone,
> I always give a hungry dog
>   A nice, fat, meaty bone.
>
> "I wouldn't drive a bobtailed horse,
>   Nor hurry up a cow,
> I ——"

Then he forgot the rest. The boys and girls were sorry. They called out, "Pig," "Goat," "Calf," "Sheep," "Hens," "Ducks," and all the other animals' names they could think of, but none of them was right, and as the boy had just made up the poetry, no one knew what the next would be. He stood for a long time staring at the ceiling, then he said, "I guess I'll have to give it up."

The children looked dreadfully disappointed. "Perhaps you will remember it by our next meeting," said the president anxiously.

"Possibly," said the boy. "But probably not. I think it is gone forever." And he went to his seat.

The next thing was to call for new members. Miss Laura got up and said she would like to join their Band of Mercy. I followed her up to the platform while they pinned a little badge on her, and everyone laughed at me. Then they sang "God Bless Our Native Land" and the president told us that we might all go home.

21

Mr. Maxwell and Mr. Harry

MR. MAXWELL wore a coat with loose pockets, and after the meeting was over, he rested on his crutches and began to slap the pockets with his hands. "No, there's nothing here today," he said. "I think I emptied my pockets before I came to the meeting."

Just as he said that, there was a loud squeal.

"Oh, my guinea pig!" he exclaimed. "I forgot him!" And he pulled out a little spotted creature a few inches long. "Poor little Derry, did I hurt you?" He soothed it very tenderly.

I stood and looked at Mr. Maxwell, for I had never seen anyone like him. He had thick curly hair and a white face, and he looked just like a girl. While I was staring at him, something peeped up out of one of his pockets and ran out its

tongue at me so fast that I could scarcely see it, and then drew
back again. I was thunderstruck. I had never seen such a creature before. It was long and thin like a boy's cane, and of a
bright green color like grass, and it had queer shiny eyes. But
its tongue was the strangest part—it came and went like
lightning. I was uneasy about it and began to bark.

"What's the matter, Joe?" said Mrs. Wood. "The pig
won't hurt you."

But it wasn't the pig I was afraid of, and I kept on barking.
And all the time that strange live thing kept sticking up its
head and putting out its tongue at me, and neither of them
noticed it.

"It's getting on toward six," said Mrs. Wood. "We must be
getting home. Come, Mr. Maxwell."

The young man put the guinea pig in his pocket, picked up
his crutches, and we started down the the sunny village street.
He left his guinea pig at his boardinghouse as we went by,
but he said nothing about the other creature, and so I knew he
did not know it was there.

I was very much taken with Mr. Maxwell. He seemed so
bright and happy in spite of his lameness, which kept him
from walking about like other young men. He looked older
than Miss Laura, and one day a week or two later, when they
were sitting on the veranda, I heard him tell her that he was
just nineteen. He told her, too, that his lameness made him
love animals. They never laughed at him, or got impatient
because he could not walk quickly. They were always good to
him, and he told her he loved all animals.

On this day as he was limping along, he said to Mrs. Wood,
"I am getting more absentminded every day. Have you heard
of my latest escapade?"

"No," she said.

"I am glad," he replied. "I was afraid that it would be all over the village by this time. I went to church last Sunday with my poor guinea pig in my pocket. He hasn't been well, and I was attending to him before church and put him in there to get warm, and then forgot about him. Unfortunately I was late, and the back seats were all full; so I had to sit farther up than I usually do. During the first hymn I happened to strike Piggy against the side of the seat. Such an earsplitting squeal as he set up! It sounded as if I was murdering him. The people stared and stared, and I had to leave church, overwhelmed with confusion."

Mrs. Wood and Miss Laura laughed. Then they got to talking about other matters that were not interesting to me; so I did not listen. But I kept close to Miss Laura, for I was afraid that green thing might hurt her. I wondered very much what its name was.

"There's something the matter with Joe," said Miss Laura when we got into the lane. "What is it, dear old fellow?" She put down her little hand, and I licked it and wished so much that I could speak.

Sometimes I wish very much that I had the gift of speech, and then at other times I see how little it would profit me, and how many foolish things I should often say. And I don't believe human beings would love animals as well, if they could speak.

When we reached the house, we got a joyful surprise. There was a trunk standing on the veranda, and as soon as Mrs. Wood saw it, she gave a little shriek.

"My dear boy!"

Mr. Harry was there, sure enough, and stepped out through

the open door. He took his mother in his arms and kissed her, then he shook hands with Miss Laura and Mr. Maxwell, who seemed to be an old friend of his. They all sat down on the veranda and talked, and I lay at Miss Laura's feet and looked at Mr. Harry. He was such a handsome young man, and had such a noble face. He was older and graver-looking than when I saw him last, and he had a light brown mustache that he did not have when he was in Fairport.

He seemed very fond of his mother and of Miss Laura, and however grave his face might be when he was looking at Mr. Maxwell, it always lighted up with a smile when he turned to them.

"What dog is that?" he said at last, his face puzzled as he pointed at me.

"Why, Harry!" exclaimed Miss Laura. "Don't you know Beautiful Joe, that you rescued from that wretched milkman?"

"Is it possible," he said, "that this well-conditioned creature is the bundle of dirty skin and bones that we nursed in Fairport? Come here, sir. Do you remember me?"

Indeed I did remember him, and I licked his hands and looked up gratefully into his face.

"You're almost handsome now," he said, caressing me with a firm, kind hand, "and of a solid build, too. You look like a fighter—but I suppose you wouldn't let him fight, even if he wanted to, Laura." He smiled and glanced at her.

"No," she said. "I don't think I should. But he can fight when the occasion requires it." And she told him about our night with Jenkins.

All the time she was speaking, Mr. Harry held me by the paws, and stroked my body over and over again. When she finished, he put his head down to me and murmured, "Good dog." I saw that his eyes were shining.

"That's a capital story! We must have it at the Band of Mercy," said Mr. Maxwell. Mrs. Wood had gone to help prepare the tea. So the two young men were alone with Miss Laura. When they had done talking about me, she asked Mr. Harry a number of questions about his college life and his trip to New York, for he had not been studying all the time he was away.

"What are you going to do with yourself, Gray, when your college course is ended?" asked Mr. Maxwell.

"I am going to settle down right here," said Mr. Harry.

"What, be a farmer?" asked his friend.

"Yes, why not?"

"Nothing, only I imagined that you would take a profession," said Mr. Maxwell. He added, "Most farmers lead such a dog's life."

"So they do," said Mr. Harry. "However, a great deal of that is their own fault. Farming, with a little effort on the farmer's part, could be made much more attractive than it is."

Mr. Maxwell smiled. "Attractive farming. Just sketch an outline of that, will you, Gray?"

"In the first place," said Mr. Harry, "I would tear out of the heart of the farmer the thing that is as firmly implanted in him as it is in the heart of his city brother—the thing that is doing more harm to our nation than anything else under the sun."

"What is that?" asked Mr. Maxwell curiously.

"The thirst for gold. The farmer wants to get rich, and he works so hard to do it that he wears himself out soul and body, and the young people around him get so disgusted with that way of getting rich that they go off to the cities to find out some other way, or at least to enjoy themselves, for I don't think many young people are animated by a desire to heap up money."

Mr. Maxwell looked amused. "There is certainly a great exodus from country places cityward," he said. "What would be your plan for checking it?"

"I would make the farm so pleasant that you couldn't hire the boys and girls to leave it. I would have them work, and work hard, too, but when their work was over, I would let them have some fun. That is what they go to the city for. They want amusement and society, and to get into some kind of a crowd when their work is done. That could be done in the country. If farmers would be contented with smaller profits and smaller farms, their houses could be nearer together. Their children would have opportunities to form societies and clubs, and that would tend to a distribution of literature. A farmer ought to take five or six papers and two or three magazines. He would find it would pay him in the long run, and there ought to be a law made compelling him to go to the post office once a day."

Mr. Maxwell burst out laughing. "Then you should make him mend his roads as well as mend his ways. I tell you, Gray, the bad roads would put an end to all these fine schemes of yours. Imagine farmers calling on each other on a dark evening after a spring freshet. I can see them mired and bogged, and the house a mile ahead of them."

"That is true," said Mr. Harry. "The road question is a serious one. Do you know how Father and I settle it?"

"No," said Mr. Maxwell.

"We keep our own roads in order," said Mr. Harry, his face serious. "Once a year, Father gets a gang of men and tackles every section of the road that borders upon our land, and our roads are the best around here. I wish the government would take up this matter of making roads and settle it. If we had good, smooth, country roads, such as they have in some parts of Europe, we would be able to travel comfortably over them all through the year, and our draft animals would last longer, for they would not have to expend so much energy in drawing their loads."

22

What Happened
at the Tea Table

FROM MY station under Miss Laura's chair, I could see that all the time Mr. Harry was speaking, Mr. Maxwell, although he spoke rather as if he was laughing at him, was yet glancing at him admiringly.

When Mr. Harry was silent, he exclaimed, "You are right, Gray! With smooth highways and plenty of schools and churches and libraries, and meetings for young people, you would make country life a paradise, and I tell you what else you would do. You would empty the slums of the cities."

"How right both you boys are," said a voice behind us, and looking around, we saw Mr. Wood standing in the doorway, gazing down proudly on his stepson and Mr. Maxwell.

Mr. Harry smiled and, getting up, he said, "Won't you have my chair, sir?"

"No, thank you. Your mother wishes us to come to tea. There are muffins, and I'm afraid they won't improve with keeping."

They all went into the dining room, and I followed them. On the way, Mr. Wood said, "Right on top of that talk of yours, Harry, I've got to tell you of another person who is going to Boston to live."

"Who is it?" said Mr. Harry.

"Lazy Dan Wilson. I've been to see him this afternoon. You know his wife is not well, and they never have quite enough to eat. He says he is going to the city, for he hates to chop wood and work, and he thinks maybe he'll get some light job there."

Mr. Harry looked grave, and Mr. Maxwell said, "He will starve, that's what he will do."

"Precisely," said Mr. Wood, spreading out his hard brown hands as he sat down at the table. "I don't know why it is, but the present generation has a marvelous way of skimming around any kind of work with their hands. They'll work their brains till they haven't got any more backbone than a caterpillar, but as for manual labor, it's old-timey and out of fashion. I wonder how these farms would ever have been carved out of the backwoods, if the old Puritans had sat down on the rocks with their noses in a lot of books, and tried to figure out just how little work they could do and yet exist."

"Now, Father," said Mrs. Wood, "you are trying to insinuate that the present generation is lazy, and I'm sure it isn't. Look at Harry. He works as hard as you do."

"Isn't that like a woman?" said Mr. Wood, with a good-natured laugh. "The present generation consists of her son, and the past of her husband. I don't think all our young people are lazy, Hattie; but how in creation, unless the Lord rains down a few farmers, are we going to support all these young lawyers and doctors that our colleges are turning out?"

"You don't mean to undervalue the advantages of a good education, do you, Mr. Wood?" said Mr. Maxwell.

"No, no. Look at Harry here. Isn't he pegging away at his studies with my hearty approval? And he's going to be nothing but a plain, common farmer. He'll be a better one than I've been, though, because he's got a trained mind. I found that out when he was a lad going to the village school. He'd lay out his little garden by geometry, and dig his ditches by algebra. Education's a help to any man. What I am trying to get at is this, that in some way or other we're running more to brains and less to hard work than our forefathers did."

Mr. Wood was beating on the table with his forefinger while he talked, and everyone was laughing at him. "When you've quite finished speechifying, John," said Mrs. Wood, "perhaps you'll serve the berries and pass the cream and sugar."

There was a great tinkling of china, and passing of dishes, and talking and laughing, and no one noticed that I was not in my usual place in the hall. I could not get over my dread of the green creature, and I had crept under the table, so that if it came out and frightened Miss Laura, I could jump up and catch it.

When tea was half over, she gave a little cry. I sprang up on her lap, and there, gliding over the table toward her, was the wicked-looking green thing. I stepped on the table, and had it by the middle before it could get to her. My hind legs were in a plate of cake, and my front ones were in a dish of jelly, and I was very uncomfortable. The tail of the green thing hung in a milk pitcher, and its tongue was still going at me, but I held it firmly and stood still.

"Drop it, drop it!" cried Miss Laura in tones of distress, and Mr. Maxwell struck me on the back. So I let the thing go, and stood sheepishly looking about me. Mr. Wood was leaning back in his chair, laughing with all his might, and Mrs. Wood was staring at her untidy table with rather a long face. Miss Laura told me to jump to the floor, and then she helped her aunt to take away the spoiled things.

I felt that I had done wrong; so I slunk out into the hall. Mr. Maxwell was sitting on the lounge, tearing his handkerchief in strips and tying them around the creature where my teeth had sunk in. I had been careful not to hurt it much, for I knew it was a pet of his. But he did not know that and scowled at me, saying, "You rascal! You've hurt my poor snake terribly."

I felt so bad to hear this that I went and stood with my head in a corner. I had almost rather be whipped than scolded. After a while, Mr. Maxwell went back into the room, and they all went on with their tea. I could hear Mr. Wood's loud, cheery voice. "The dog did quite right. A snake is mostly a poisonous creature, and his instinct told him to protect his mistress. Where is he? Joe, Joe!"

I would not move till Miss Laura came and spoke to me. "Dear old dog," she whispered. "You knew the snake was there all the time, didn't you?" Her words made me feel better, and I followed her to the dining room, where Mr. Wood made me sit beside him and eat scraps from his hand all through the meal.

Mr. Maxwell had got over his ill humor and was chatting in a lively way. "Good dog," he said. "I was cross to you, and I beg your pardon. It always riles me to have any of my pets injured. You didn't know the poor snake was only after something to eat. Mrs. Wood has pinned him in my pocket so he won't come out again. Do you know where I got that snake, Mrs. Wood?"

"No," she said, "you never told me."

"It was across the river by Blue Ridge," he said. "One day last summer I was out rowing. I was getting very hot, and so I tied my boat in the shade of a big tree. Some village boys were in the woods, and when I heard a great noise, I went to see what it was all about. They were a Band of Mercy boys who had found a country boy beating a snake to death. They were remonstrating with him for his cruelty, telling him that some kinds of snakes were a help to the farmer, and destroyed large numbers of field mice and other vermin. The boy was obstinate. He had found the snake, and he insisted upon his right to kill it, and they were having rather a lively time when I appeared. I persuaded them to make the snake over to me. Apparently it was already dead. Thinking I might revive it, I put it on some grass in the bow of the boat. It lay there motionless for a long time, and I picked up my oars and started for home. I had got halfway across the river, when I turned around and saw that the snake was gone. It had just dropped into the water, and was swimming toward the bank we had left. I turned and followed it.

"It swam slowly and with evident pain, lifting its head every few seconds high above the water, to see which way it was going. On reaching the bank it coiled itself up. I took it up carefully, carried it home, and nursed it. It soon got better and has been a pet of mine ever since."

After tea was over Mrs. Wood said she thought a fire would be pleasant. So they lighted the sticks of wood in the open grate, and all sat around the blazing fire.

Mr. Maxwell tried to get me to make friends with the little snake that he held in his hands toward the blaze, and now that I knew it was harmless I was not afraid of it. But it did not like me, and put out its funny little tongue whenever I looked at it.

23

Trapping Wild Animals

A s you all know," said Mr. Wood, looking thoughtfully into the fire, "I was brought up in the eastern part of Maine. We often used to go to New Brunswick for our sport. Moose were our best game. Did you ever see one, Laura?"

"No, Uncle," she said.

"Well, when I was a boy there was no more beautiful sight to me in the world than a moose with his dusky hide, long legs, branching antlers, and shoulders standing higher than a horse's. Their legs are so long that they can't eat close to the ground. They browse on the tops of plants, and the tender shoots and leaves of trees. They walk among the thick underbrush, carrying their horns adroitly to prevent catching in the branches, and they step so well, and aim so true, that you'll

156

scarcely hear a twig fall as they go through the forest.

"They're timid creatures, most of the time. But sometimes they'll attack with hoofs and antlers whatever comes in their way. They hate mosquitoes, and when they're tormented by mosquitoes, it's just as well to be careful about approaching them. Like all other creatures, the Lord has put into them a wonderful amount of sense. When a female moose has her one or two fawns, she goes into the deepest part of the forest, or swims to an island in a large lake, and stays there until the fawns are able to look out for themselves.

"Well, we used to like to catch a moose, and we had different ways of doing it. One way was to snare the animal. We'd make a loop in a rope and hide it on the ground under the dead leaves in one of their paths. This was connected with a young sapling whose top was bent down. When the moose stepped on the loop, it would release the sapling, and the sapling would bound up, catching him by the leg. These snares were always set deep in the woods, and we couldn't visit them very often. Sometimes the moose would be there for days, raging and tearing around and scratching the skin off his legs. That was very cruel, and I wouldn't catch a moose in that way now for a hundred dollars.

"Another way was to hunt them on snowshoes with dogs. In February and March the snow was deep, and the crust was hard enough to carry men and dogs. Moose don't go together in herds. In the summer they wander about the forest, and in the autumn they come together in small groups. They select one or two hundred acres where there is plenty of heavy undergrowth, and there they usually confine themselves.

"Any of these places where there were several moose, we called a moose yard. We went through the woods till we got on to the tracks of some of the animals belonging to it. Then the dogs smelled them and went ahead to start them. If I shut my eyes now I can see one of our moose hunts—the moose running and plunging through the snow crust, and occasionally rising up and striking at the dogs that hung onto his flanks and legs; the hunters' rifles going crack, crack, crack, sometimes killing or wounding dogs as well as moose. That, too, was cruel.

"Two other ways we had of hunting moose—calling and stalking. The calling was done in this way: We took a bit of birch bark and rolled it up in the shape of a horn. We took this horn and started out, either on a bright moonlight night, or just at evening, or early in the morning. The man who carried the horn hid himself and then began to make a lowing sound with it, like a female moose. He had to do it pretty well to deceive them. Away in the distance some moose would hear it and with answering grunts would start to come to it. If a young male moose was coming, he'd mind his steps, I can assure you, on account of fear of the old ones. But if it was an old fellow, you'd hear him stepping out bravely, rapping his horns against the trees and plunging into any water that came in his way. When he got pretty near, he'd stop to listen, and then the caller had to be very careful and put his trumpet down close to the ground, so as to make a lower sound. If the moose felt doubtful, he'd turn and go. If not, he'd come on, and unlucky for him if he did, for he got a warm reception, either from the rifles in our hands as we lay hid near the caller, or from someone stationed at a distance.

"In stalking them, we crept on them the way a cat creeps on a mouse. In the daytime a moose is usually lying down. We'd find their tracks and places where they'd been nipping off the ends of branches and twigs, and follow them up. They easily take the scent of men, and we'd have to keep well to the leeward. Sometimes we'd come upon them lying down, but if in walking along we'd broken a twig, or made the slightest noise, they'd think it was one of their mortal enemies, a bear, and they'd be up and away. Their sense of hearing is very keen, but they're not so quick to see. A fox is like that, too. His eyes aren't equal to his nose.

"Stalking is the most merciful way to kill a moose. Then they haven't the fright and suffering of the chase."

"I don't see why they need to be killed at all," said Mrs. Wood. "If I knew that forest back of the mountains was full of wild creatures, I think I'd be glad of it, and not want to hunt them. That is, if they were harmless and beautiful creatures like the deer."

"You're a woman," said Mr. Wood, "and women are more merciful than men. Men want to kill and slay. They're like the man who said, 'What a fine day it is! Let's go out and kill something.' "

"Please tell us some more about the dogs that helped you catch the moose, Uncle," said Miss Laura. I was sitting up very straight beside her, listening to every word Mr. Wood said, and she was fondling my head.

"Well, Laura, when we camped out on the snow and slept on spruce boughs while we were after the moose, the dogs used to be a great comfort to us. They slept at our feet and kept us warm. Poor brutes, they mostly had a rough time of it. They enjoyed the running and chasing as much as we did, but when it came to broken ribs and sore heads, it was another matter. Then the porcupines bothered them. Our dogs would never learn to let porcupines alone. If they were going through the woods where there were no signs of moose and found a porcupine, they'd kill it. The quills would get in their mouths and necks and chests, and we'd have to pull out the nasty things."

"Poor brutes," said Mrs. Wood. "I wonder you took them along."

"It was good sport to see the dogs when we were hunting a bear with them," Mr. Wood went on. "Bears are good runners, and when dogs get after them, there is great skirmishing. They nip the bear behind, and when the bear turns, the dogs run like mad, for a hug from a bear means sure death to a dog."

"Were there many bears near your home, Mr. Wood?" asked Mr. Maxwell.

"Lots of them. More than we wanted. They used to bother us fearfully about our sheep and cattle. Everybody hated bears, and hadn't much pity for them. Still, they were getting their meat as other wild animals do, and we'd no right to set such cruel traps for them as the steel ones. It was a great event in the neighborhood when a bear was caught. Whoever caught him blew a horn, and the men and boys came trooping together to see the sight. I've known them to blow that horn on a Sunday morning, and I've seen the men turn their backs on the meetinghouse to go and see the bear."

"Was there no more merciful way of catching them than by the leg in those steel traps?" asked Miss Laura.

"Oh, yes, by the deadfall—that is by driving heavy sticks into the ground, and making a boxlike place, open on one side, where two logs were so arranged with other heavy logs upon them that, when the bear seized the bait, the upper log fell down and crushed him to death. Another way was to fix a bait in a certain place, with cords tied to it, and the cords were fastened to triggers of guns placed at a little distance. When the bear took the bait, the guns went off, and he shot himself. When hit by the log or shot, the bear died swiftly and that was more merciful than being caught by the teeth of a steel trap and sometimes staying there in agony for days.

"One day when I was in the woods, I looked through the trees and spied a bear. He was standing up on his hind legs, snuffing in every direction, and just about the time I spied him, he spied me. I had no dog or gun, and so I thought I had better be getting home to my dinner. I was a small boy then, and the bear, probably thinking I'd be a mouthful for him anyway, began to come after me in a leisurely way. I can see myself now going through those woods—hat gone, jacket flying, arms out, eyes rolling over my shoulder every little while to see if the bear was gaining on me. He was a benevolent-looking old fellow, and his face seemed to say, 'Don't hurry, little boy.' I soon got away from him, but I made up my mind then that it was more fun to be the chaser than the chased."

24

The Rabbit and the Hen

Mr. wood looked slowly around the little circle before the fire. He smiled and said, "I have talked enough for one evening. Everyone looks tired, and so I think I'll send you to bed."

"Very well," said Miss Laura, and the others nodded in agreement. She said good-night and went upstairs. Mr. Wood turned to Mr. Maxwell. "You're going to stay all night with us, aren't you?"

"So Mrs. Wood says," replied the young man, smiling.

"Of course," said Mrs. Wood. "I couldn't think of letting you go back to the village on such a night as this. It's raining cats and dogs—but I mustn't say that, or there'll be no getting you to stay. I'll go and prepare your old room next to Harry's." And she bustled away.

The two young men went to the pantry for doughnuts and milk, and Mr. Wood stood gazing down at me. "Good dog," he said. "You look as if you sensed that talk tonight. Come get a bone, and then away to bed."

He gave me a very large mutton bone, and I held it in my mouth and watched him opening the woodshed door. I love human beings, and the saddest time of day for me is when I have to be separated from them while they sleep.

"Now, go to bed and rest well, Beautiful Joe," said Mr. Wood. "And if you hear any stranger around the house, run out and bark. Don't be chasing wild animals in your sleep, though. They say a dog is the only animal that dreams. I wonder whether it's true?" Then he went into the house and shut the door.

I had a sheepskin to lie on, and a very good bed it made. I slept soundly for a long time. Then I waked up and found that, instead of rain pattering against the roof, and darkness everywhere, it was quite light. The rain was over and the moon was shining beautifully. I ran to the door and looked out. It was almost as light as day. The moon made it very bright all around the house and the farm buildings, and I could look all about and see that there was no one stirring. I took a turn around the yard and walked around to the side of the house to glance up at Miss Laura's window. I always did this several times through the night, just to see if she was quite safe. I was on my way back to my bed when I saw two small, white things moving away down the lane. I stood on the veranda and watched them. When they came nearer, I saw that there was a white rabbit hopping up the road, followed by a white hen.

It seemed to me a very strange thing for these creatures to

be out this time of night, and why were they coming to Dingley Farm? This wasn't their home. I ran down the road and stood in front of them.

Just as soon as the hen saw me, she fluttered in front of the rabbit and, spreading out her wings, she clucked angrily and acted as if she would peck my eyes out if I came a step nearer.

I saw that they were harmless creatures and, remembering my adventure with the snake, I stepped aside. Besides that, I knew by their smell that they had been near Mr. Maxwell; so perhaps they were after him.

They understood quite well that I would not hurt them, and passed by me. The rabbit went ahead again and the hen fell behind. It seemed to me that the hen was sleepy and didn't like to be out so late at night, and was only following the rabbit because she thought it was her duty.

He was going along in a very queer fashion, putting his nose to the ground, and rising up on his hind legs and sniffing the air, first on this side and then on the other, and his nose going, going, all the time.

He smelled all around the house till he came to Mr. Maxwell's room at the back. It opened on the veranda by a glass door, and the door stood ajar. The rabbit squeezed himself in, and the hen stayed out. She watched for a while, and when he didn't come back, she flew up to the back of a chair that stood near the door and put her head under a wing.

I went back to my bed, for I knew they would do no harm. Early in the morning when I was walking around the house, I heard a great shouting and laughing from Mr. Maxwell's room. He and Harry had just discovered the hen and the rabbit, and Mr. Harry was calling his mother to come and look at them. The rabbit had slept at the foot of the bed.

Mr. Harry was chaffing Mr. Maxwell very much, and was telling him that anyone who entertained him was in for a traveling menagerie. They had a great deal of fun over it, and Mr. Maxwell said that he had had that pretty white hen as a pet for a long time in Boston. Once when she had some little chickens, a frightened rabbit that was being chased by a dog ran into the yard. In his terror he got right under the hen's wings, and she sheltered him and pecked at the dog's eyes, and kept him off till help came. The rabbit belonged to a neighbor's boy, and Mr. Maxwell bought it from him. From the day the hen protected him, she became his friend and followed him everywhere.

I did not wonder that the rabbit wanted to see his master. There was something about that young man that made dumb animals just delight in him. When Mrs. Wood mentioned this to him, he said, "I don't know why they should. I don't do anything to fascinate them."

"You love them," she said, "and they know it. That is the reason."

25

Happy Horses

FOR A GOOD while after I went to Dingley Farm I was very shy of the horses, for I was afraid they might kick me. However, they all had such good faces, and looked at me so kindly, that I was beginning to get over my fear of them.

Fleetfoot, Mr. Harry's colt, was my favorite, and one afternoon when Mr. Harry and Miss Laura were going out to see him, I followed them. Fleetfoot was amusing himself by rolling over and over on the grass under a tree, but when he saw Mr. Harry, he gave a shrill whinny and, running to him, began nosing about his pockets, looking for sugar.

"Wait a bit," said Mr. Harry, holding him by the forelock. "Let me introduce you to this young lady, Miss Laura Morris. I want you to make her a bow." He gave the colt some sign, and immediately he began to paw the ground and shake his head.

Mr. Harry laughed and went on. "Here is her dog, Joe. I want you to like him, too. Come here, Joe." I was not at all afraid, for I knew Mr. Harry would not let him hurt me. So I stood in front of him, and for the first time had a good look at him. They called him the colt, but he was really a full-grown horse, and had already been put to work. He was of a dark chestnut color, and had a well-shaped body and a long, handsome head, and I never saw, in the head of a man or beast, a more beautiful pair of eyes than that colt had—large, full, brown eyes that turned on me almost as a person's would.

I looked at him very earnestly and wagged my body, and lifted myself on my hind legs toward him. He seemed pleased and put down his nose to sniff at me.

Mr. Harry pulled some lumps of sugar out of his pocket and, giving them to Miss Laura, told her to put them on the palm of her hand and hold them out to Fleetfoot. The colt ate the sugar and all the time eyed her with his quiet, observing glance that made her exclaim, "What a wise-looking colt!"

"He is like an old horse," said Mr. Harry. "When he hears a sudden noise, he stops and looks all about him to find an explanation."

"He has been well trained," said Miss Laura.

"I have brought him up carefully." Mr. Harry smiled and threw his arm over the colt's neck. "We've been comrades, haven't we, Fleetfoot? We're going out in the buggy this afternoon. Will you come?"

"Where are you going?" asked Miss Laura.

"Just for a short drive back of the river to collect some money for Father. I'll be home long before teatime."

"Yes, I should like to go," said Miss Laura. "I'll go to the house and get my other hat."

"Come on, Fleetfoot," said Mr. Harry. And he led the way from the pasture, the colt following behind with me. I waited about the veranda, and in a short time Mr. Harry drove up to the front door. The buggy was black and shining, and Fleetfoot had on a silver-mounted harness that made him look very fine. I stood by him, and as soon as he saw that Miss Laura and Mr. Harry had seated themselves, he acted as if he wanted to be off. Mr. Harry spoke to him and away he went, and I raced down the lane by his side. He had a beautiful even gait and went very swiftly. Mr. Harry kept speaking to him to check him.

"You don't like to have him go too fast, do you?" said Miss Laura. "Why?"

"Because so much of the farm work must be done at a walk. Plowing, teaming, and drawing produce to market, and going up and down hills." Mr. Harry smiled. "But I do let you trot sometimes, don't I, Fleetfoot? How about a spin now, my boy?"

Away we went on a bit of level road. Fleetfoot had no checkrein on his beautiful neck, and when he trotted, he could hold his head in an easy, natural position. With his wonderful eyes and flowing mane and tail, and his glossy, reddish-brown body, I thought that he was the handsomest horse I had ever seen. He loved to go fast, and when Mr. Harry spoke to him to slow up again, he tossed his head with impatience. But he was too sweet-tempered to disobey. In all the years that I have known Fleetfoot, I have never once seen him refuse to do as his master told him.

"You have forgotten your whip, haven't you, Harry?" I

heard Miss Laura say, as we jogged slowly along, and I ran by the buggy panting and with my tongue hanging out.

"I never use one," said Mr. Harry. "A properly trained horse needs none."

"I suppose Fleetfoot never balks," said Miss Laura.

"No," replied Mr. Harry. "At least, he hasn't yet."

"Fleetfoot has had a happy life, hasn't he?" said Miss Laura, looking admiringly at him. "How did he get to like you so much, Harry?"

"I broke him in after a fashion of my own. Father gave him to me, and the first time I saw him on his feet, I went up carefully and put my hand on him. His mother was rather shy of me, for we hadn't had her very long, and it made him shy, too, and so I soon left him. The next time I stroked him; after that I put my arm around him. Soon he acted like a big dog. I could lead him about by a strap, and I made a little halter and a bridle for him. I did not let him do too much work. Colts are like boys—a boy shouldn't do a man's work, but he had exercise every day, and I trained him to draw a light cart behind him. I used to do all kinds of things to accustom him to sudden or unusual sounds."

"You like horses better than any other animals, don't you, Harry?" asked Miss Laura.

"I believe I do, though I am very fond of that dog of yours. I think I know more about horses than dogs. Have you noticed Scamp very much?"

"Oh, yes. I've often watched her. She is such an amusing little creature."

"She's the most interesting horse we've got, that is, after Fleetfoot. Father got her from a man who couldn't manage her, and she came to us with a legion of bad tricks. Father has

taken solid comfort in breaking her of them. She is his pet among our stock now. And she loves him, too, and seems attached to all the other horses, especially Fleetfoot and Cleve and Pacer."

"I love to go for drives with Cleve and Pacer," said Miss Laura. "They are so steady and good. Uncle says they are the steadiest horses he has. Did you hear the story that Uncle told last evening about them? I don't think you were around then. It was about stealing the oats."

"Cleve and Pacer never steal," said Mr. Harry. "Don't you mean Scamp? She's the thief."

"No, it was Pacer that stole. He got out of his box, Uncle says, and found two bags of oats, and he took one in his teeth and dropped it before Cleve, and ate the other himself. Uncle was so amused that he let them eat a long time, and stood and watched them."

"That *was* a clever trick," said Mr. Harry. "Father must have forgotten to tell me. Those two horses have been mates ever since I can remember, and I believe if they were separated, they'd pine away and die. You have noticed how low the partitions are between the boxes in the horse stable. Father says you wouldn't put a lot of people in separate boxes in a room where they couldn't see each other, and horses are just as fond of company as we are. Cleve and Pacer are always nosing each other. A horse has a long memory. Father has had horses recognize him that he has been parted from for twenty years. Speaking of their memories reminds me of another good story about Pacer that I never heard till yesterday, and that I would not talk about to anyone but you and Mother. Father wouldn't write me about it, for he never will put a line on paper where anyone's reputation is concerned."

26

The Box of Money

THIS STORY," said Mr. Harry, "is about one of the hired men we had last winter, whose name was Jacobs. He was a cunning fellow, with a hang-dog look and a great cleverness at stealing farm produce from Father on the sly, and selling it. Father knew perfectly well what he was doing, and was wondering what would be the best way to deal with him, when one day something happened that brought matters to a climax and quickly settled the trouble.

"Father had to go to Sudbury for farming tools, and took Pacer and the cutter. There are two ways of going there—one the Sudbury Road, and the other the old Post Road, which is longer and seldom used. The snow wasn't deep, and he wanted to inquire after an old man who had been robbed and half frightened to death a few days before. He was a miserable old creature, known as Miser Jerrold, and he lived alone with his daughter. He had saved a little money through the years that he always kept in a box under his bed.

"When Father got near the place, he was astonished to see by Pacer's actions that he had been on this road before, and recently, too. Father is so sharp about horses that they never do a thing he doesn't attach a meaning to. So he let the reins hang a little loose and kept his eye on Pacer. The horse went along the road, and when Father didn't direct him, he turned into the lane leading to the house. There was an old red gate at the end of it, and he stopped in front of the gate and waited for Father to get out. Then he passed through but, instead of going up to the house, turned around and stood with his head toward the road.

"Father never said a word, but he was doing a lot of thinking. He went into the house and found the old man sitting over the fire, rubbing his hands and half crying about 'the few poor dollars' that he said were stolen from him. Father had never seen him before, but he knew the old man had the name of being half silly. Question him as much as he liked, Father could make nothing of him. The daughter said they had gone to bed at dark the night her father was robbed. She slept upstairs, and he down below. About ten o'clock she heard him scream and, running downstairs, she found him sitting up in bed and the window wide open. He said a man had sprung in upon him, stuffed the bedclothes into his mouth, and, dragging his box from under the bed, had made off with it. She ran to the door and looked out, but there was no one to be seen. It was dark and snowing a little, and so no traces of footsteps were to be seen in the morning.

"Father found that the neighbors were dropping in to keep the old man company, and so he drove on to Sudbury, and then returned home. When he got back, he said Jacobs was hanging about the stable in a nervous kind of way, and said he wanted to speak to him. Father said very good, but put the horse in first. Jacobs unhitched, and Father sat on one of the stable benches and watched him till he came lounging along with a straw in his mouth, and said he'd made up his mind to go West, and he'd like to set off at once.

"Father said again, very good, but first he had a little account to settle with him, and he took out of his pocket a paper where he had jotted down, as far as he could, every quart of oats, and every bag of grain, and every quarter of a dollar of market money that Jacobs had defrauded him of. Father said the fellow turned all the colors of the rainbow, for he thought he had covered up his tracks so cleverly that he would never be found out. Then Father said, 'Sit down, Jacobs, for I have to have a long talk with you.' He had him there about an hour, and when he finished, the fellow was completely broken down.

"Father told him that there were just two courses in life for a young man to take, and he had taken the wrong one. He was a smart young fellow, and if he turned right around now, there was a chance for him. If he didn't there was nothing but the State's prison ahead of him, for he needn't think he was going to gull and cheat all the world, and never be found out. Father said he'd give him all the help in his power, if he had his word that he'd try to be an honest man. Then he tore up the paper, and said there was an end of his indebtedness to him.

"Jacobs is only a young fellow, twenty-three or thereabouts,

and Father said he sobbed like a baby. Then, without looking at him, Father gave an account of his afternoon's drive,
just as if he was talking to himself. He said that Pacer never
to his knowledge had been on that road before, and yet he
seemed perfectly familiar with it, and that he stopped and
turned, all ready to leave again quickly instead of going up to
the door, and then he looked over his shoulder and started on
a run down the lane the minute Father's foot was in the cutter
again. In the course of his remarks, Father mentioned the fact
that on Monday, the evening that the robbery was committed,
Jacobs had borrowed Pacer to go to the Junction, but had
come in with the horse steaming and looking as if he had been
driven a much longer distance than that. Father said that
when he finished, Jacobs had sunk down all in a heap on the
stable floor, with his hands over his face. Father left him to
have it out with himself, and went to the house.

"The next morning Jacobs looked just the same as usual,
and went about with the other men doing his work, but saying nothing about going West. Late in the afternoon a farmer
going by hailed Father and asked if he'd heard the news. Old
Miser Jerrold's box had been left on his doorstep some time
during the night, and he'd found it in the morning. The
money was all there, but the old fellow was so cute that he
wouldn't tell anyone how much it was. The neighbors had
persuaded him to bank it, and he was coming to town the
next morning with it, and that night some of them were going to help him mount guard over it. Father told the men at
milking time, and he said Jacobs looked as unconscious as
possible. However, from that day there was a change in him.
He never told Father in so many words that he'd resolved to
be an honest man, but his actions spoke for him. He had been

a kind of sullen, unwilling fellow, but now he turned handy and obliging, and it was a real trial to Father to part with him when Jacobs finally decided to leave."

Miss Laura was intensely interested in his story. "Where is he now, Cousin Harry?" she asked eagerly. "What has become of him?"

Mr. Harry laughed as he said, "Jacobs married Old Miser Jerrold's daughter, and Father and Mother went to the wedding. Father gave the bridegroom a yoke of oxen, and Mother gave the bride a lot of household linen, and I believe they're as happy as the day is long. Jacobs is improving the farm that was going to rack and ruin, and I hear he is going to build a new house."

"Harry," exclaimed Miss Laura, "can't you drive me over to see them?"

"Yes, indeed. Mother often drives over to take them little things, and we'll go, too, sometime."

"Where did you say we were going now?" asked Miss Laura as we crossed the bridge over the river.

"A little way back here in the woods," he replied. "There's an Englishman on a small clearing that he calls Penhollow. Father loaned him some money three years ago, and he won't pay either interest or principal."

"I think I've heard of him," said Miss Laura. "Isn't he the man the boys call Lord Chesterfield?"

"That's the man," said Harry. "He is a character if ever I saw one. He lives alone, only coming occasionally to the village for supplies, and though he is poorer than poverty, he despises every soul within a ten-mile radius of him, and looks upon us as no better than an order of thrifty, well-trained lower animals."

"Why is that?" asked Miss Laura in surprise.

"He is a gentleman, Laura, and we are only common people. My father can't hand a lady in and out of a carriage as Lord Chesterfield can, nor can he make so grand a bow, nor does he put on evening dress for a late dinner, and we never go to the opera nor to the theatre, and know nothing of polite society, nor can we tell exactly whom our great-great-grandfather sprang from. I tell you, there is a gulf between us and that Englishman wider than the one young Curtius leaped into."

Miss Laura was laughing merrily. "How funny that sounds, Harry. So he despises you." And she glanced at her good-looking cousin, and his handsome buggy and well-kept horse, and then burst into another peal of laughter.

Mr. Harry laughed, too. "It does seem absurd. Sometimes when I pass him jogging along to town in his rickety old cart, and look at his pale, cruel face, and know that he is a broken-down gambler and man of the world, and yet considers himself infinitely superior to me—a young man in the prime of life, with a good constitution and happy prospects—it makes me turn away to hide a smile. Here we are at the entrance to the mansion of Penhollow. I must get out and open the gate that will admit us to the winding avenue."

We had to go very slowly up a narrow, rough road. The bushes scratched and scraped against the buggy, and Mr. Harry looked very much annoyed. Finally he said, "We have arrived at last, thank goodness."

There was a small grass clearing in the midst of the woods. Chips and bits of wood were littered about, and across the clearing was a roughly built house of unpainted boards. The front door was propped open by a stick. Some of the panes of glass in the windows were broken, and the house had a melancholy, dilapidated look. I thought that I had never seen such a sad-looking place.

"It seems as if there is no one about," said Mr. Harry, with a puzzled face. "Will you hold Fleetfoot, Laura, while I go and see?"

He drew the buggy up near a small log building that had evidently been used for a stable, and I lay down beside it and watched Miss Laura.

27

A Neglected Stable

I DIDN'T know what it was, but I knew there was something wrong somewhere. So did Fleetfoot.

"Joe," said Miss Laura, "why don't you and Fleetfoot stand still? Is there a stranger about?"

Barking, I asked her to excuse me, and I ran to the other side of the log hut.

"You won't find anything in that ramshackle old place, Beautiful Joe," said Miss Laura, who had climbed down out of the buggy and followed me.

However, she pulled open the rough door of the hut and looked in. "Is anyone here?" she asked in her clear sweet voice. There was no answer, except a low moaning sound.

I shall never forget seeing my dear Miss Laura going into

that wet and filthy log house, her face a picture of pain and horror. There were two rough stalls in it; in the first one was tied a cow, with a calf lying beside her. How thin she was! Miss Laura gave one cry of pity, and seizing a little penknife from her pocket, she hacked at the rope that tied the cow to the manger, and cut it so that the cow could lie down. The first thing the poor cow did was to lick her calf, but it was quite dead.

Miss Laura then went into the other stall to see if there was any creature there. There had been a horse. There was now a lean, gaunt-looking animal lying on the ground, with a heavy rope knotted round his neck and fastened to his empty rack. Miss Laura cut his rope, too, and led him outside the stall, speaking kindly to him. He was the weakest, most distressed-looking animal I ever saw.

All this had taken only a few minutes, and just after she got the horse out, Mr. Harry appeared. He came out of the house with a slow step that quickened to a run when he saw Miss Laura.

"Laura!" he exclaimed. "What are you doing?" Then he stopped and looked at the horse, not in amazement, but very sorrowfully. "Barron is gone," he said, and crumpling up a piece of paper, he put it in his pocket. "What is to be done for these animals? There is a cow, isn't there?"

"Yes," said Miss Laura.

"Laura," said Mr. Harry, "will you go home and tell Father that Barron has run away and left a starving pig, cow, and horse here? Joe will look after you. Meanwhile I will go back to the house and heat some water."

It seemed only a few minutes later that we drove into our yard. Adele came out to meet us. Mr. Wood was gone to the meadow, she said, and Mrs. Wood had a cold and chills and was in bed and asleep now.

"Then you will help me, Adele, like a good girl," said Miss Laura, hurrying into the house. "We've found a sick horse and cow, and I must take them something to eat."

For a few minutes, Miss Laura and Adele flew about the kitchen, and then we set off again. Miss Laura took me in the buggy, for I was out of breath and wheezing greatly. I had to sit on the seat beside her, for the bottom of the buggy and the back were full of eatables for the poor sick animals, bran mash, vegetables, oats, hay, and corn, and milk for the pig. Just as we drove into the road, we met Mr. Wood. Miss Laura said a few words to him, and with a very grave face he got in beside her. Mr. Harry was waiting at the gate for us, and when he saw Miss Laura, he said, "Why did you come back again? You'll be tired out."

"I thought I might be of some use," she said.

"Bless the child," said Mr. Wood, taking the things out of the buggy. "She's thought of everything, even the salt."

For more than an hour they were fussing over the animals. Then they came in and sat down. The inside of the house was as untidy as the outside. There was no upstairs to it, only a large room with a dirty curtain stretched across it. On one side was a low bed with a heap of clothes on it, a chair, and a washstand. On the other was a stove, a table, a shaky rocking chair that Miss Laura sat down on somewhat gingerly, a few hanging shelves with some dishes and books on them, and two or three boxes.

On the walls were tacked some pictures of grand houses and ladies and gentlemen in fine clothes, and Miss Laura said that some of them were noble people.

"Well, I'm glad this particular nobleman has left us," said Mr. Wood, seating himself on one of the boxes. "If nobleman he is. I should call him, in plain English, a scoundrel. Did Harry show you his note?"

"No, Uncle," said Miss Laura.

"Read it aloud," said Mr. Wood. "I'd like to hear it once more."

Miss Laura read:

> "J. Wood, Esquire. Dear Sir: It is a matter of great regret to me that I am suddenly called away from my place at Penhollow, and will, therefore, not be able to do myself the pleasure of calling on you and settling my little account. I sincerely hope that the possession of my livestock, which I make entirely over to you, will more than reimburse you for any trifling expense which you may have incurred on my account. If it is any gratification to you to know that you have rendered a slight assistance to the son of one of England's noblest noblemen, you have it. With expressions of the deepest respect, and hoping that my stock may be in good condition when you take possession,
>
> "I am, dear sir, ever devotedly yours,
>   "Howard Algernon Leduc Barron"

Miss Laura dropped the paper. "Uncle, did he leave those animals to starve?"

"Didn't you notice," said Mr. Wood grimly, "that there wasn't a wisp of hay inside that shanty, and that where the poor beasts were tied up the wood was gnawed and bitten by them in their torture for food? Wouldn't he have sent me that note, instead of leaving it here on the table, if he'd wanted me to know? The note isn't dated, but I judge he's been gone five or six days. He intended me to come here and find every animal dead."

They left the room, and Miss Laura sat turning the sheet of paper over and over, with a kind of horror in her face. It was a very dirty piece of paper, but by and by she made a discovery. She took it in her hand and went outdoors. She called to her cousin, "Harry, will you look at this?"

He took the paper from her, and said, "That is a crest shining through the dust and grime, probably that of his own family. We'll have it cleaned, and it will enable us to find the villain. You want him punished, don't you?"

"Yes, I do," said Miss Laura frankly.

"Well, my dear girl," he said, "Father and I are with you. If we can hunt Barron down, we'll do it."

Miss Laura saw that Mr. Wood and Mr. Harry were doing all that could be done for the cow and horse. So she wandered down to a hollow at the back of the house, where the Englishman had kept his pig. Just now, the animal looked more like a greyhound than a pig, his legs were so long and his nose so sharp. Hunger, instead of making him stupid like the horse and cow, had made him more lively. Mr. Harry said he had been raging around his pen digging the ground with his snout, when he had found him.

Now, his hunger satisfied, he was gazing contentedly at his little rough trough that was still half full of good milk.

In a short time we went home with Mr. Wood. Mr. Harry was going to stay all night with the sick animals, and his mother would send him things to make him comfortable. Later in the evening she sent one of the men over with a whole box full of things for her boy, and a nice hot supper, done up for him in a covered dish.

When the man came home, he said that Mr. Harry would not sleep in the Englishman's dirty house, but had slung a hammock out under the trees. It was a lonely place for him out there in the woods, and his mother said that she would be glad when the sick animals could be driven to their own farm.

28

The End
of the Englishman

In a few days, thanks to Mr. Harry's constant care, the horse and cow were able to walk. It was a mournful procession that came into the yard at Dingley Farm. The hollow-eyed horse, the lean cow, and the funny, thin little pig, staggered along in a shaky fashion. Though it was only a mile or two from Penhollow to Dingley Farm, they were exhausted, and fell on their comfortable beds in the clean barn.

Miss Laura was so delighted they had all lived that she did not know what to do. Her eyes were bright and shining, and she went from one to another with a happy face. The little pig, that Mr. Harry had christened "Daddy Long Legs," had been washed, and he lay in a corner of his neat little pen and surveyed his clean trough and abundance of food with the air of a prince.

Mr. Wood had a number of pigs, and after a while Daddy was put in with them, and a fine time he had of it making friends with the the other little grunters. They were often let out in the pasture or orchard, and when they were there, I could always single out Daddy from among them, because he was the smartest. It was amusing to see him when a storm was coming on, running about in a state of great excitement, carrying little bundles of straw in his mouth to make himself a bed. He was a white pig, and was always kept clean. Mr. Wood said it was wrong to keep pigs dirty. They like to be clean as well as other animals, and if they are kept so, they are much more contented.

The cow, poor, unhappy creature, never as long as she lived on Dingley Farm, lost a strange, melancholy look from her eyes. I have heard it said that animals forget past unhappiness, and perhaps some of them do, but this one would often stand chewing her cud and looking away in the distance, thinking of her dead calf, I am sure. Even the farm hands called her "Old Melancholy," and soon she got to be known by that name, or Mel, for short.

The horse they named "Scrub," because he could never be, under any circumstance, anything but a broken-down, plain-looking animal. He was put into the horse stable in a stall next to Fleetfoot, and as the partition was low, they could look at each other. Miss Laura petted him a great deal. She often took apples to the stable, and Fleetfoot would throw up his beautiful head and look reproachfully over the partition at her, for she always stayed longer with Scrub than with him, and Scrub always got a larger share of whatever good thing was going.

Poor old Scrub. I think he loved Miss Laura. He was a stupid sort of horse and always acted as if he was blind. If he was in the field, he never seemed to know her till she was right under his pale-colored eyes. Then he would be delighted to see her. He was not blind, though, for Mr. Wood said he was not. He said he had probably not been an over-bright horse to start with, and had been made more dull by cruel usage.

As for the Englishman, the master of these three animals, a very strange thing happened to him. Mr. Wood and Mr. Harry were so very angry with him that they said they would leave no stone unturned to have him punished, or at least to have it known what a villain he was. They sent the paper with the crest on it to Boston. Some people there wrote to England and found out that it was the crest of a noble and highly esteemed family, and some earl was at the head of it. They were all honorable people in this family except one man, a nephew, not a son, of the late earl. He was the black sheep of them all. As a young man he had led a wild and wicked life, and had ended by forging the name of one of his friends, so that he was obliged to leave England and take refuge in America. By the description of this man, Mr. Wood knew that he must be Mr. Barron. So he wrote to these English people and told them what a wicked thing their relative had done in leaving his animals to starve. In a short time he got an answer from them which was very proud and, at the same time, very touching. It came from Mr. Barron's cousin, and he said quite frankly that he knew his relative was a man of evil habits, but it seemed as if nothing could be done to reform him. His family was accustomed to send a quarterly allowance to him, on condition that he led a quiet life in some retired place, but their last remittance to him was lying unclaimed in Boston, and they thought he must be dead. Could Mr. Wood tell them anything about him?

Mr. Wood looked very thoughtful when he got this letter. Then he said, "Harry, how long is it since Barron ran away?"

"About eight weeks," said Mr. Harry.

"That's strange," said Mr. Wood. "The money these people sent him would get to Boston just a few days after he left here. He is not the man to leave it long unclaimed. Something must have happened to him. Where do you suppose he would go from Penhollow?"

"I have no idea, sir," said Mr. Harry.

"And how would he go?" said Mr. Wood. "He did not leave Riverdale Station, because he would have been spotted by some of his creditors."

"Perhaps he would cut through the woods to the Junction," said Mr. Harry.

"Just what he would do," said Mr. Wood, slapping his knee. "I'll be driving over there tomorrow to see Thompson, and I'll make inquiries."

Mr. Harry spoke to his father the next night when he came home, and asked if he had found out anything.

"Only this," said Mr. Wood. "There's no one answering to Barron's description who has left Riverdale Junction within a twelvemonth. He must have struck some other station. We'll let him go. The Lord will punish him."

Months passed, and nothing was heard of him. Late in the autumn, after Miss Laura and I had got back to Fairport, Mrs. Wood wrote her about the Englishman. It seemed some Riverdale lads were beating about the woods for lost cattle, and had come upon an old stone quarry that had been disused for years. On one side was a smooth wall of rock, many feet deep. On the other side the ground and rock were broken away, and it was quite easy to get into the quarry. They found that one of their cows had fallen into this deep pit, over the steep side of the quarry. Of course the poor creature was dead, but the boys went down anyway, and there they found the skeleton of a man. Nearby was the walking stick that Barron always carried.

Mrs. Wood said that her husband had written about the finding of Mr. Barron's body to his English relatives, and had received a letter from them, thanking Mr. Wood for his interest. They were having their money sent from Boston to Mr. Wood, and they wished him to expend it in the way he thought best fitted to counteract the evil effects of their relative's doings in Riverdale. When this money came, it amounted to some hundreds of dollars. Mr. Wood would have nothing to do with it. He handed it over to the Band of Mercy, and they formed what they called the "Barron Fund," which they drew upon when they wanted money for buying and circulating humane literature.

29

A Talk About Sheep

Miss LAURA was very much interested in the sheep on Dingley Farm. There was a flock in the orchard near the house that she often went to see. She always carried roots and vegetables to them, turnips particularly, for they were very fond of them. Mr. Wood called them his little Southdowns, and he said he loved his sheep, for they were such gentle and inoffensive creatures.

One day when he came into the kitchen inquiring for salt, Miss Laura said, "Is it for the sheep?"

"Yes," he replied. "I am going up to the woods pasture to examine my Shropshires."

"You would like to go, too, Laura," said Mrs. Wood. "Take your hands right away from that cake. I'll finish frosting it for you. Run along and get your broad-brimmed hat. It's very hot."

Miss Laura danced out into the hall and back again, and soon we were walking back of the house, along a path that led us through the fields to the pasture. When we reached the gate that opened into the pasture, Mr. Wood let Miss Laura go through and then closed it behind her. He said, "You are looking at that gate. You want to know why it is so long, don't you?"

"Yes, Uncle," she said, "but I don't like to ask so many questions."

"Ask as many as you like," he said good-naturedly. "I don't mind answering them. Have you ever seen sheep pass through a gate or a door?"

"Oh, yes, often."

"And how do they act?"

"Oh, so silly, Uncle. They hang back, and one waits for another. And, finally, they all try to go through the gate at once."

"Precisely. When one goes they all want to go, even if it is to jump into a bottomless pit. Many sheep are injured by overcrowding, and so I have my gates and doors very wide. Now, let us call them up."

There wasn't one in sight. But Mr. Wood lifted up his voice and cried, "Ca nan, nan, nan!" Quickly, black faces began to peer out from among the bushes, and little black legs carrying white bodies came hurrying up the stony paths from the cooler parts of the pasture. Oh, how glad they were to get the salt! Mr. Wood let Miss Laura spread it on some flat rocks. Then they sat down on a log under a tree and watched the sheep eating it and licking the rocks when it was all gone.

Miss Laura sat fanning herself with her hat and smiling at them. "You funny, woolly things," she said. "You're not so stupid as some people think you are. Lie still, Joe. If you show yourself, they may run away."

I crouched behind the log, and only lifted my head occasionally to see what the sheep were doing. Some of them went back to the cool woods, but most of them did not want to leave Mr. Wood.

"You know, my child," said Mr. Wood, stroking the top of one lamb's head, "my grandfather would open his eyes in amazement, and ask me if I was an old woman petting her cats, if he were alive and could know the care I give my sheep. He used to let his flock run till the fields were covered with snow, and bite as close as they liked, till there wasn't a scrap of feed left. Then he would give them an open shed to run under, and throw down their hay outside. Grain they scarcely knew the taste of. That they would fall off in flesh, and half of them lose their lambs in the spring, was an expected thing. He would say I had them kennelled, if he could see my big closed sheds, with the sunny windows, that my flock spends the winter in. I even house them during the bad fall storms. They can run out again. Indeed, I like to get them in, and have a snack of dry food, to break them in to it. They are in and out of those sheds all winter. You must go in, Laura, and see the self-feeding racks. On bright winter days they get a run in the cornfields. Cold doesn't hurt sheep, but heavy rain soaks their fleeces.

"With my way I seldom lose a sheep, and they're the most

profitable stock I have. If I could not keep them, I think I'd give up farming. Last year my lambs netted me eight dollars each. The fleeces of the ewes average eight pounds and sell for two dollars each."

"How many sheep have you, Uncle?" asked Miss Laura.

"Only fifty, now. Twenty-five here and twenty-five down below in the orchard. I've been selling a good many this spring."

"These sheep are larger than those in the orchard, aren't they?" said Miss Laura.

"Yes. I keep those few Southdowns for their fine quality. I don't make as much on them as I do on these Shropshires. For an all-around sheep I like the Shropshire. It's good for mutton, for wool, and for rearing lambs."

"These sheep are a long way from the house," said Miss Laura. "Don't dogs attack them?"

"No. Since I had that brush with Windham's dog, I've trained the sheep to go and come with the cows. It's a queer thing, but cows that will run from a dog when they are alone will fight him if he meddles with their calves or with the sheep. There's not a dog around that would dare to come into this pasture, for he knows the cows would be after him with lowered horns and a business look in their eyes. The sheep in the orchard are safe enough, for they're near the house, and if a strange dog came around, Joe would settle him, wouldn't you, Joe?"

He went on, "By and by the Southdowns will be changed up here, and the Shropshires will go down to the orchard. I like to keep one flock under my fruit trees. You know there is an old proverb, 'The sheep has a golden hoof.' They save me the trouble of plowing. I haven't plowed my orchard for ten years, and don't expect to plow it for ten years more. Then your Aunt Hattie's hens are so obliging that they keep me from the worry of finding ticks at shearing time. All the year round, I let them run among the sheep, and they nab every tick they see."

"How closely sheep bite!" exclaimed Miss Laura, pointing to one that was nibbling almost at his master's feet.

"Very close, and they eat a good many things that cows don't relish—bitter weeds and briars and shrubs and the young ferns that come up in the spring."

"I wish I could get hold of one of those dear little lambs," said Miss Laura. "See that sweet little blackie back in the alders. Could you not coax him up?"

"He wouldn't come here," said her uncle kindly. "But I'll try to get him for you."

He rose, and after several efforts, succeeded in capturing the black-faced creature and bringing him up to the log. He was very shy of Miss Laura, but Mr. Wood held him firmly and let her stroke his head.

"You call him little," said Mr. Wood. "If you put your arm around him, you'll find he's a pretty substantial lamb. He was born in March, and this is the last of July. He'll be shorn next month and think he's quite grown-up. Poor little fellow! He had quite a struggle for life.

"The sheep were turned out to pasture in April. They can't bear confinement as well as the cows, and as they bite closer, they can be turned out earlier. They get on well by having food rations of corn in addition to the grass, which is thin and poor so early in the spring. This young creature was running by his mother's side, rather a weak-legged, poor specimen of a lamb. Every night the flock was put under shelter, for the ground was cold, and though the sheep might not suffer from lying out-of-doors, the lambs would get chilled.

"One night this fellow's mother went astray, and as Ben neglected to make the count, she wasn't missed. I'm always anxious about my lambs in the spring and often get up in the night to look after them. That night I went out about two o'clock. I took it into my head, for some reason or other, to count them. I found a sheep and a lamb missing, took my lantern and Bruno, who was good at tracking sheep, and I hope will be again, and started out. Bruno barked and I called, and the foolish creature came to me, the little lamb staggering after her.

"I wrapped the lamb in my coat, took it to the house, made a fire, and heated some milk. Your Aunt Hattie heard me and got up. She put some ground ginger in the milk, and forced it down the lamb's throat. Then we wrapped an old blanket round him and put him near the stove, and the next evening he was ready to go back to his mother. I petted him all through April, and gave him extras—different kinds of meal—till I found what suited him best. Now he does me credit."

"Dear little lamb," said Miss Laura, patting him. "How can you tell him from the others, Uncle?"

"I know all their faces, Laura. A flock of sheep is just like a crowd of people. They all have different expressions."

"They all look alike to me," said Miss Laura.

"I daresay. You are not accustomed to them. Do you know how to tell a sheep's age?"

"No, Uncle."

"Here, open your mouth, Cosset," he said to the lamb

that he still held. "At one year they have two teeth in the center of the jaw. They get two more teeth every year up to five years. Then we say they have a 'full mouth.' After that you can't tell their age exactly by the teeth. Now, run back to your mother." He let the lamb go.

"Do they always know their own mothers?" asked Miss Laura as she watched the lamb run away.

"Usually. Sometimes a ewe will not own her lamb. In that case we tie them up in a separate stall till she recognizes her lamb. Do you see that sheep over there by the blueberry bushes—the one with the very pointed ears?"

"Yes, Uncle," said Miss Laura.

"That lamb by her side is not her own. Hers died and we took its fleece and wrapped it around a twin lamb that we took from another ewe, and gave it to her. She soon adopted it. Now, come this way, and I'll show you our movable feeding troughs."

He got up from the log, and Miss Laura followed him to the fence.

"These big troughs are for the sheep," said Mr. Wood. "Those shallow ones in the enclosure are for the lambs. See, there is just room enough for them to get under the fence. You should see the small creatures rush to them whenever we appear with their oats or wheat or bran, or whatever we are going to give them. If they are going to the butcher, they get corn meal and oil meal. Whatever it is, they eat it up clean. I don't believe in cramming animals. I feed them as much as is good for them, and not any more. Now, you go sit down over there behind those bushes with Joe, and I'll attend to business."

Miss Laura found a shady place, and I curled myself up

beside her. We sat there a long time, but we did not get tired, for it was amusing to watch the sheep and lambs. After a while Mr. Wood came and sat down beside us. He talked some more about sheep-raising. Then he said, "You may stay here longer if you like, but I must get down to the house."

"What are you going to do now?" asked Miss Laura, jumping up.

"Oh, more sheep business. I've set out some young trees in the orchard, and unless I get chicken wire around them, my sheep will be barking them for me."

"I've seen them," said Miss Laura, "standing up on their hind legs and nibbling at the trees, taking off every shoot they can reach."

"They don't hurt the old trees," said Mr. Wood. "But the young ones have to be protected. It pays me to take care of my fruit trees, for I get a splendid crop from them, thanks to the sheep."

"Good-bye, little lambs and dear old sheep," said Miss Laura, rising to go back with her uncle.

After this Miss Laura and I often went up to the pasture to see the sheep and the lambs. We used to get into a shady place where they could not see us, and watch them. One day I got a great surprise about the sheep. I had heard so much about their meekness that I never dreamed they would fight. But it turned out that they did, and they went about it in such a businesslike way that I could not help smiling at them. I suppose that, like most other animals, they had a spice of wickedness in them.

On this day a quarrel arose between two sheep. But instead of running at each other like two dogs, they went a long distance apart, and then came rushing at each other with lowered

heads. Their object seemed to be to break each other's skulls.
But Miss Laura soon stopped them by calling out and fright-
ening them apart.

I thought that the lambs were more interesting than the
sheep. Sometimes they fed quietly by their mothers' sides,
and at other times they all huddled together on the top of
some flat rock or in a bare place, and seemed to be talking to
each other with their heads close together. Suddenly one
would jump down and start for the bushes or the other side
of the pasture. They would all follow pell-mell. Then in a
few minutes they would come rushing back again. It was
pretty to see them having a good time together.

30

A Jealous Ox

M<small>R. WOOD</small> had a dozen calves that he was raising, and Miss Laura sometimes went up to the stable to see them. Each calf was in a crib, and it was fed with milk. They had gentle, patient faces and beautiful eyes, and looked very meek, as they stood quietly gazing about them or sucking away at their milk. They reminded me of big, gentle dogs.

I never got a very good look at them in their cribs, but one day when they were old enough to be let out, I went up with Miss Laura to the yard where they were kept. Such queer, ungainly, large-boned creatures they were! And such a good time they were having, running and jumping and throwing up their heels!

Mrs. Wood was with us, and she said it was not good for

calves to be closely penned after they got to be a few weeks old. They were better for getting out and having a frolic. She stood beside Miss Laura for a long time, watching the calves and laughing a great deal at their awkward gambols. They wanted to play, but they did not seem to know how to use their limbs.

They were lean calves, and Miss Laura asked her aunt why all the nice milk they had taken had not made them any fatter.

"The fat will come all in good time," said Mrs. Wood. "A fat calf makes a poor cow, and a fat, small calf isn't profitable or fit for sending to the butcher. It's better to have a bony one and fatten it. If you come here next summer, you'll see a fine show of young cattle, with fat sides and big, open horns and a good coat of hair. Come and see the cow stable. John has just had it whitewashed. It's so fresh and clean."

Miss Laura took her aunt's arm, and I walked slowly behind them.

The cow stable was a long building, well built and with no chinks in the walls, as Jenkins's stable had. There were large windows where the afternoon sun came streaming in, and a number of ventilators and a great many stalls. A pipe of water ran through the stalls from one end of the stable to the other. The floor was covered with sawdust and leaves, and the ceiling and tops of the walls were whitewashed. Mrs. Wood said that her husband would not have the walls a glare of white right down to the floor, because he thought it injured the animals' eyes. So the lower parts of the walls were stained a dark brown color.

There were doors at each end of the stable, and just now they stood open and a gentle breeze was blowing through.

But Mrs. Wood said that when the cattle stood in the stalls, both doors were never allowed to be open at the same time. Mr. Wood was most particular to have no drafts blowing upon his cattle. He would not have them chilled, and he would not have them overheated. One thing was as bad as the other. And during the winter they were never allowed to drink icy water. He took the chill off the water for his cows, just as Mrs. Wood did for her hens.

"You know, Laura," Mrs. Wood went on, "that when cows are kept dry and warm, they eat less than when they are wet and cold. They are so warm-blooded that if they are cold, they have to eat a great deal to keep up the heat of their bodies, and so it pays better to house and feed them well. They like quiet, too. I never knew that till I married your uncle. On our farm, the boys always shouted and screamed at the cows when they were driving them, and sometimes made them run. They're never allowed to do that here."

"I have noticed how quiet this farm seems," said Miss Laura. "You have so many men about, and yet there is so little noise."

"Your uncle whistles a great deal," said Mrs. Wood. "Have you noticed that? He whistles when he's about his work, and he has a calling whistle that nearly all of the animals know, and the men run when they hear it. You'd see every cow in his stable turn its head, if he whistled in a certain way outside. He says that he got into the way of doing it when he was a boy and went for his father's cows. He trained them so that he'd just stand in the pasture and whistle, and they'd come to him.

"I believe the first thing that inclined me to him was his clear, happy whistle. I'd hear him from our house away down

on the road, jogging along with his cart or driving in his
buggy. He says there is no need of screaming at any animal.
It only frightens and angers them. They will mind much
better if you speak clearly and distinctly. He says there is
only one thing an animal hates more than to be shouted
at, and that is to be crept on—to have a person sneak up to it
and startle it. John says many a man is kicked because he
comes up to his horse like a thief. A startled animal's first
instinct is to defend itself. A dog will spring at you, and a
horse will let his heels fly. John always speaks or whistles
to let the stock know when he's approaching."

"Where is Uncle this afternoon?" asked Miss Laura.

"Oh, up to his eyes in hay. He's even got one of the oxen
harnessed to a hay cart."

"I wonder whether it's Duke?" said Miss Laura.

"Yes, I saw the star on his forehead," replied Mrs. Wood.

"I don't know when I have laughed at anything as much
as I did at him the other day," said Miss Laura. "Uncle asked
me if I had ever heard of such a thing as a jealous ox, and
I said no. He said, 'Come to the barnyard, and I'll show you
one.'

"The oxen were both there, Duke with his broad face
and Bright so much sharper and more intelligent-looking.
Duke was drinking at the trough there, and Uncle said, 'Just
look at him. Isn't he a great, fat, self-satisfied creature, and
doesn't he look as if he thought the world owed him a living, and he ought to get it?' Then he got the card and went
up to Bright, and began scratching him. Duke lifted his head
from his trough and stared at Uncle, who paid no attention
to him but went on carding Bright, and stroking and petting
him. Duke looked so angry! He left the trough, and with

the water dripping from his lips, went up to Uncle, and gave
him a push with his horns. Still Uncle took no notice, and
Duke almost pushed him over. Then Uncle left off petting
Bright and turned to him. He said Duke would have treated
him roughly, if he hadn't. I never saw a creature look as satisfied as Duke did, when Uncle began to card him. Bright
didn't seem to care, and only gazed calmly at them."

"I've seen Duke do that again and again," said Mrs. Wood.
"He's the most jealous animal that we have, and it makes
him perfectly miserable to have your uncle pay attention to
any animal but him. What queer creatures these dumb brutes
are. They're pretty much like us in most ways. They're jealous and resentful, and they can love or hate equally well—
and forgive, too, for that matter; and suffer, and so patiently,
too. Where is the human being that would put up with the
tortures that animals endure and yet come out so patient?"

"Nowhere," said Miss Laura in a low voice.

"And there doesn't seem to be an animal," Mrs. Wood
went on, "no matter how ugly or repulsive it is, but what has
some lovable qualities."

Miss Laura put her arm affectionately around her aunt
and said, "I love to be with you, dear Auntie, because you
have the same feeling for dumb animals that I have. I love
them, and I want to stop and talk to every one I see. Sometimes I worry poor Bessie Drury, and I'm so sorry, but I can't
help it. She says, 'What makes you so silly, Laura?'"

Miss Laura was standing just where the sunlight shone
through her light brown hair and made her face all in a glow.
I thought she looked more beautiful than I had ever seen
her, and I think Mrs. Wood thought the same thing. She
put both hands on Miss Laura's shoulders.

"Laura," she said earnestly, "there are enough cold hearts in the world. Don't you ever stifle a warm or tender feeling toward a dumb creature. That is your chief attraction, my child—your love for everything that breathes and moves. Tear out the selfishness from your heart, if there is any there, but let the love and pity stay. And now let me talk a little more to you about the cows. I want to interest you in dairy matters. This stable is new since you were here, and we've made a number of improvements. Do you see those bits of rock salt in each stall? They are for the cows to lick whenever they want to. Now, come here, and I'll show you what we call 'The Black Hole.' "

It was a tiny stable off the main one, and it was very dark and cool. "Is this a place of punishment?" asked Miss Laura in surprise.

Mrs. Wood laughed heartily. "No, no. A place of pleasure! Sometimes when the flies are very bad and the cows are brought into the yard to be milked and the flies settle on them, they are nearly frantic. And though they are the best cows in New Hampshire, they will kick a little. When they do, those that are the worst are brought in here to be milked where there are no flies. The others have big strips of cotton laid over their backs and tied under them, and the men brush their legs with tansy tea, or water with a little carbolic acid in it. That keeps the flies away, and the cows know well that it is done for their comfort, and stand quietly till the milking is over. I must ask John to have their nightdresses put on sometime for you to see. Harry calls them 'sheeted ghosts,' and they do look queer enough standing all round the barnyard robed in white."

31

In the Cow Stable

Isn't it a strange thing," said Miss Laura, "that a little thing like a fly can cause so much annoyance to animals as well as to people? Sometimes when I am trying to get more sleep in the morning, their little feet tickle me so that I am nearly frantic and have to fly out of bed to chase them away."

"You shall have some netting to put over your bed," said Mrs. Wood. "But suppose, Laura, you had no hands to brush away the flies. Suppose your whole body was covered with them, and you were tied up somewhere and could not get loose. I can't imagine more exquisite torture myself. Last summer the flies here were dreadful. It seems to me that they are getting worse and worse every year, and worry the animals more. I believe it is because the birds are getting thinned out all over the country. There are not enough of them to catch the flies. John says that the next improvement we make on the farm is to wire gauze at all the stable windows and screen doors to keep the little pests from the horses and cattle.

"One afternoon last summer, Mr. Maxwell's mother came for me to go for a drive with her. The heat was intense, and when we got down by the river, she proposed getting out of the phaeton and sitting under the trees to see if it would be any cooler. She was driving a horse that she had got from the hotel in the village, a roan horse that was clipped and checkreined and had his tail docked. I wouldn't drive behind a tailless horse now. Then I wasn't so particular. However, I made her unfasten the checkrein before I'd set foot in the carriage.

"Well, I thought that horse would go mad. He'd tremble and shiver and look so pitifully at us. The flies were nearly eating him up. Then he'd start a little. Mrs. Maxwell had a weight at his head to hold him, but he could easily have dragged that. He was a good dispositioned horse, and he didn't want to run away, but he could not stand still. I soon jumped up and slapped him, and rubbed him till my hands were dripping wet. The poor brute was so grateful and would keep touching my arm with his nose. Mrs. Maxwell sat under the trees fanning herself and laughing at me, but I didn't care. How could I enjoy myself with a dumb creature writhing in pain before me?

"A docked horse can neither eat nor sleep comfortably in the fly season. In one of our New England villages they have a sign up, 'Horses taken in to grass. Long tails, one dollar and fifty cents. Short tails, one dollar.' And it just means that the short-tailed ones are taken cheaper because they are so bothered by the flies that they can't eat much, while the long-tailed ones are able to brush them away, and eat in peace. I read the other day of a Buffalo coal dealer's horse that was in such an agony through flies that he committed suicide. You know animals will do that. I've read of horses and dogs drowning themselves. This horse had been clipped, and his tail was docked, and he was turned out to graze. The flies stung him till he was nearly crazy. He ran up to a picket fence, and sprang up on one of the sharp spikes. There he hung, making no effort to get down. Some men saw him do it, and they said it was a clear case of suicide.

"I would like to have the power to take every man who cuts off a horse's tail, and tie his hands and turn him out in a field in the hot sun, with little clothing on, and plenty of flies about. Then we would see if he wouldn't sympathize with the poor dumb beast. It's the most senseless thing in the world, this docking fashion. They've a few flimsy arguments about a horse with a docked tail being stronger-backed, like a short-tailed sheep, but I don't believe a word of it. The horse was made strong enough to do the work he's got to do, and man can't improve on him. Docking is a cruel, wicked thing.

"Now, there's a ghost of an argument in favor of check-reins, on certain occasions. A fiery young horse can't run away, with an overdrawn check, and in speeding horses a checkrein will make them hold their heads up and keep them from choking. But I don't believe in raising colts in a way to make them fiery, and I wish there wasn't a race horse on the face of the earth. So if it depended on me, every kind of checkrein would go. It's a pity we women can't vote, Laura. We'd certainly do away with a good many abuses."

Miss Laura smiled, but it was a very faint, almost unhappy smile, and Mrs. Wood said hastily, "Let us talk about something else. Did you ever hear that cows will give less milk on a dark day than on a bright one?"

"No, I never did," said Miss Laura.

"Well, they do. They are most sensitive animals. One finds out all manner of curious things about animals if he makes a study of them. Cows are wonderful creatures, I think, and so grateful for good usage that they return every scrap of care given them, with interest. Have you ever heard anything about dehorning, Laura?"

"Not much, Auntie. Does Uncle approve of it?"

"No, indeed. He'd just as soon think of cutting off their tails, as of dehorning them. He says he guesses the Creator knew how to make a cow better than he does. Sometimes I tell John that his argument doesn't hold good, for a man in some ways can improve on nature. In the natural course of things, a cow would be feeding her calf for half a year, but we take it away from her, and raise it as well as she could and get an extra quantity of milk from her in addition. I don't know what to think myself about dehorning. Mr. Windham's cattle are all polled, and he has an open space in his barn for them, instead of keeping them in stalls, and he says they're more comfortable and not so confined. I suppose in sending cattle to sea, it's necessary to take their horns off, but when they're going to be turned out to grass, it seems like mutilating them. Our cows couldn't keep the dogs away from the sheep if they didn't have horns. Their horns are their means of defense."

"Do your cattle stand in these stalls all winter?" asked Miss Laura.

"Oh, yes, except when they're turned out in the barnyard, and then John usually has to send a man to keep them moving, or they'd take cold. Sometimes on very fine days they get out all day. You know cows aren't like horses. John says they're like great milk machines. You've got to keep them quiet, only exercising them enough to keep them in health. If a cow is hurried or worried, or chilled or heated, it stops her milk yield. And bad usage poisons it. John says you can't take a stick and strike a cow across the back without her milk being that much worse, and as for drinking the milk that comes from a cow that isn't kept clean, you'd better throw it away and drink water."

Miss Laura looked at her aunt and said earnestly. "That is where you folk who live in the country have the advantage over us city dwellers. You know where your milk comes from and just how clean and pure and fine it is, because you raise the cows and do the milking yourselves. But we who take our milk from dairies are not always so sure, even though our milk is inspected."

"You city people are imposed upon with regard to your milk," said Mrs. Wood. "I should think you'd be poisoned with the treatment your cows receive. Even when your milk is examined, you can't tell whether it is pure or not. In New York the law only requires thirteen per cent of solids in milk. That's absurd, for you can feed a cow on swill and still get fourteen per cent of solids in it. Oh, you city people are queer!"

Miss Laura laughed heartily. "What a prejudice you have against large towns, Auntie."

"Yes, I have," said Mrs. Wood honestly. "I often wish we could break up a few of our cities and scatter the people through the country. Look at the lovely farms all about here, some of them with only an old man and woman on them. The boys are off to the cities, slaving in stores and offices, and growing pale and sickly. It would have broken my heart if Harry had taken to city ways. I had a plain talk with your uncle when I married him, and said, 'Now, my boy's only a baby, and I want him to be brought up so that he will love the country life. How are we going to do it?'

"Your uncle looked at me with a sly twinkle in his eye and said I was a pretty fair specimen of a country girl, and so suppose we brought up Harry the way I'd been brought up. I knew he was only joking, yet I got quite excited. 'Yes,' I said, 'do as my father and mother did. Have a farm about twice as large as you can manage. Don't keep a hired man. Get up at daylight and slave till dark. Never take a holiday. Have the girls do the housework and take care of the hens and help pick the fruit, and make the boys tend the colts and the calves, and put all the money they make in the bank. Don't take any papers, for they would waste their time reading them, and it's too far to go to the post office oftener than once a week. And—' but I don't remember the rest of what I said. Anyway, your uncle burst into a roar of laughter. 'Hattie,' he said, 'my farm's too big. I'm going to sell some of it, and enjoy myself a little more.' That very week he sold fifty acres, and he hired an extra man, and got me a good girl, and twice a week he left his work in the afternoon and took me for a drive.

"Harry held the reins in his tiny fingers, and John told him that Dolly, the old mare we were driving, should be called his, and the very next horse he bought should be called his, too, and he should name it and have it for his own; and he would give him five sheep, and he should have his own bank book and keep his accounts. Harry understood, mere baby though he was, and from that day he loved John as his own father. If my father had had the wisdom that John has, his boys wouldn't be the one a poor lawyer and the other a poor doctor in two different cities; and our farm wouldn't be in the hands of strangers. It makes me sick to go back there."

Mrs. Wood was silent for a little while after she made this long speech, and Miss Laura said nothing. I took a turn or two up and down the stable, thinking of many things. No matter how happy human beings seem to be, they always have something to worry them. I was sorry for Mrs. Wood, for her face had lost the happy look it usually wore. However, she soon forgot her trouble, and said, "Now, I must go and get the tea. This is Adele's afternoon out."

"I'll come, too," said Miss Laura, "for I promised her I'd make the biscuits for tea this evening and let you rest." They both sauntered slowly down the plank walk to the house, and I followed them.

32

Our Return Home

In OCTOBER, the most beautiful of all the months, we were obliged to go back to Fairport. Miss Laura could not bear to leave the farm, and her face got very sorrowful when anyone spoke of her going away. Still, she had become well and strong and was as brown as a berry, and she said that she knew she ought to go home and get back to her lessons.

Mr. Wood called October the golden month. Everything was quiet and still, and at night and in the morning the sun had a yellow, misty look. The trees in the orchard were loaded with fruit, and some of the leaves were floating down, making a soft covering on the ground.

In the garden there were a great many flowers in bloom, in flaming red and yellow colors. Miss Laura gathered bunches of them every day to put in the parlor. One day when she was arranging them, she said regretfully, "They will soon be gone. I wish it could always be summer."

"You would get tired of it," said Mr. Harry, who had come up softly behind her. "There's only one place where we could stand perpetual summer, and that's in heaven."

"Do you suppose that it will always be summer there?" said Miss Laura, turning around and looking at him with a smile.

"I don't know. I imagine it will be, but I don't think anybody knows much about it. We've got to wait."

Miss Laura's eyes fell on me. "Harry," she said, "do you think that dumb animals will go to heaven?"

"I shall have to say again, I don't know," he replied. "Some people hold that they do. In a Michigan paper, the other day, I came across one writer's opinion on the subject. He says that among the best people of all ages have been some who believed in the future life of animals. Homer and the later Greeks, some of the Romans and early Christians held this view—the last believing that God sent angels in the shape of birds to comfort sufferers for the faith. St. Francis called the birds and beasts his brothers. Dr. Johnson believed in a future life for animals, as also did Wordsworth, Shelley, Coleridge, Jeremy Taylor, Agassiz, Lamartine, and many Christian scholars.

"It seems as if they ought to have some compensations for their terrible sufferings in this world. Then to go to heaven, animals would only have to take up the thread of their lives here. Man is a god to the lower creation. Joe worships you, much as you worship your Maker. Dumb animals live in and for their masters. They hang on our words and looks, and are dependent on us in almost every way. For my part, and looking at it from an earthly point of view, I wish with all my heart that we may find our dumb friends in paradise."

"And in the Bible," said Miss Laura, "animals are often spoken of. The dove and the raven, the wolf and the lamb, and the leopard, and the cattle that God says are his, and the little sparrow that can't fall to the ground without our Father's knowing it."

"Still, there's nothing definite about their immortality," said Mr. Harry. "However, we've got nothing to do with that. If it's all right for them to be in heaven, we'll find them there. All we have to do now is to deal with the present, and the Bible plainly tells us that 'a righteous man regardeth the life of his beast.' "

"I think I would be happier in heaven if dear old Joe were there," said Miss Laura, looking wistfully at me. "He has been such a good dog. Just think how he has loved and protected me. I think I should be lonely without him."

"That reminds me of some poetry, or rather doggerel," said Mr. Harry, "that I cut out of a newspaper for you yesterday." He drew from his pocket a little slip of paper, and read this:

> "Do doggies gang to heaven, Dad?
> Will oor auld Donald gang?
> For noo to tak' him, Faither, wi' us,
> Wad be maist awfu' wrang."

There were several other verses, telling how many kind things old Donald the dog had done for his master's family, and then it closed with these lines:

> "Without are dogs. Eh, Faither, man,
> 'Twould be an awfu' sin

To leave oor faithfu' doggie *there*,
He's certain to win in.
"Oor Donald's no like ither dogs,
He'll *no* be lockit oot,
If Donald's no let into heaven,
I'll no gang there one foot."

"My sentiments exactly," said a merry voice from behind Miss Laura and Mr. Harry, and looking up they saw Mr. Maxwell. He was holding out one hand to them, and in the other kept back a basket of large pears that Mr. Harry promptly took from him and offered to Miss Laura.

"I've been dependent upon animals for the most part of my comfort in this life," said Mr. Maxwell, "and I shan't be happy without them in heaven. I don't see how you would get on without Joe, Miss Morris, and I want my birds and my snake and my horse—how can I live without them? They're almost all my life here."

"If some animals go to heaven and not others, I think that the dog has the first claim," said Miss Laura. "He's the friend of man—the oldest and best. Have you ever heard the legend about him and Adam?"

"No," said Mr. Maxwell.

"Well, when Adam was turned out of paradise, all the animals shunned him, and he sat bitterly weeping with his head between his hands, when he felt the soft tongue of some creature touching him. He took his hands from his face, and there was a dog that had separated himself from all the other animals, and was trying to comfort him. He became the chosen friend and companion of Adam, afterward of all men."

"There is another legend," said Mr. Harry, "about our Saviour and a dog. Have you ever heard it?"

"We'll tell you that later," said Mr. Maxwell, "when we know what it is."

Mr. Harry showed his white teeth in an amused smile and began: "Once upon a time our Lord was going through a town with his disciples. A dead dog lay by the wayside, and everyone that passed along flung some offensive epithet at him. Eastern dogs are not like our dogs, and seemingly there was nothing good about this loathsome creature, but as our Saviour went by, He said gently, 'Pearls cannot equal the whiteness of his teeth.' "

"What was the name of that old fellow," said Mr. Maxwell abruptly, "who had a beautiful swan that came every day for fifteen years to bury its head in his bosom and feed from his hand, and would go near no other human being?"

"Saint Hugh, of Lincoln. We heard about him at the Band of Mercy the other day," said Miss Laura.

"I should think that he would have wanted to have that swan in heaven with him," said Mr. Maxwell. "What a beautiful creature it must have been. Speaking about animals going to heaven, I daresay some of them would object to going, on account of the company that they would meet there. Think of the dog kicked to death by his master, the horse driven into his grave, the thousands of cattle starved to death on the plains—will they want to meet their owners in heaven?"

"According to my reckoning, their owners won't be there," said Mr. Harry. "I firmly believe that the Lord will punish every man or woman who ill-treats a dumb creature just as surely as he will punish those who ill-treat their fellow creatures. If a man's life has been a long series of cruelties to dumb animals, do you suppose that he would enjoy himself in heaven, which will be full of kindness to everyone? Not he. He'd rather be in the other place, and there he'll go, I fully believe."

"When you've quite disposed of all your fellow creatures and the dumb creation, Harry, perhaps you will condescend to go into the orchard and see how your father is getting on with picking the apples," said Mrs. Wood, joining Miss Laura and the two young men, her eyes twinkling and sparkling with amusement.

"The apples will keep, Mother," said Mr. Harry, putting his arm around her. "I just came in for a moment to get Laura. Come, Maxwell, we'll all go."

"And not another word about animals," Mrs. Wood called after him. "Laura will go crazy some day through thinking of their sufferings, if someone doesn't do something to stop her."

Miss Laura turned around suddenly. "Dear Aunt Hattie," she said, "you must not say that. I am a coward, I know, about hearing of animals' pains, but I must get over it. I want to know how they suffer. I *ought* to know, for when I get to be a woman, I am going to do all I can to help them."

"And I'll join you," said Mr. Maxwell, stretching out his hand to Miss Laura. She did not smile, but looking very earnestly at him, she held it clasped in her own. "You will help me to care for them, will you?" she said.

"Yes, I promise," he said gravely. "I'll give myself to the service of dumb animals, if you will."

"And I, too," said Mr. Harry in his deep voice, laying his hand across theirs. Mrs. Wood stood looking at their fresh, eager, young faces, with tears in her eyes. Just as they all stood silently for an instant, the old village clergyman came into the room from the hall. He must have heard what they said, for before they could move he had laid his hands on their three brown ones.

"Bless you, my children," he said. "God will lift up the light of his countenance upon you, for you have given yourselves to a noble work. In serving dumb creatures, you are ennobling the human race."

Then he sat down in a chair and looked at them. He was a venerable old man, and had long white hair, and the Woods thought a great deal of him. He had come to get Mrs. Wood to make some nourishing dishes for a sick woman in the village, and while he was talking to her, Miss Laura and the two young men went out of the house. They hurried across the veranda and over the lawn, talking and laughing, and enjoying themselves as only happy young people can, and with not a trace of their seriousness of a moment before on their faces.

They were going so fast that they ran right into a flock of geese that were coming up the lane. They were driven by a little boy called Tommy, the son of one of Mr. Wood's farm laborers, and they were chattering and gabbling, and seemed very angry.

"What's all this about?" said Mr. Harry, stopping and looking at the boy. "What's the matter with your feathered charges, Tommy, my lad?"

"If it's the geese you mean," said the boy, half crying and looking very much put out, "it's all them nasty potatoes. They won't keep away from them."

"So the potatoes chase the geese, do they?" said Mr. Maxwell teasingly.

"No, no!" said the child pettishly. "Mr. Wood sets me to watch the geese, and they runs in among the buckwheat and the potatoes, and I tries to drive them out, and they doesn't want to come, and I has to switch their feet, and I hates to do it, 'cause I'm a Band of Mercy boy."

"Tommy, my son," said Mr. Maxwell solemnly, "you will go right to heaven when you die, and your geese will go with you."

"Hush, hush," said Miss Laura. "Don't tease him." Putting her arm on the child's shoulders, she said, "You are a good boy, Tommy, not to want to hurt the geese. Let me see your switch, dear."

He showed her a little stick he had in his hand, and she said, "I don't think you could hurt them much with that, and if they will be naughty and steal the potatoes, you have to drive them out. Take some of my pears and eat them, and you will forget your trouble." The child took the fruit, and Miss Laura and the two young men went on their way, smiling and looking over their shoulders at Tommy. He stood in the lane, devouring his pears and keeping one eye on the geese that had gathered a little in front of him and were gabbling noisily and having a kind of indignation meeting, because they had been driven out of the potato field.

Tommy's father and mother lived in a little house down near the road. Mr. Wood never had his hired men live in his own house. He had two small houses for them to live in, and they were required to keep them as neat as Mr. Wood's own house was kept. He said that he didn't see why he should keep a boarding house, if he was a farmer, nor why his wife should wear herself out waiting on strong, hearty men that had just as soon take care of themselves. If one of his men was unmarried, he boarded with the married one, but slept in his own house.

On this October day we found Mr. Wood hard at work under the fruit trees. He had a good many different kinds of apples. Enormous red ones, and long yellow ones that they called pippins, and little brown ones, and smooth-coated sweet ones, and bright red ones, and others, more than I could mention. Miss Laura often pared one and cut off little bits for me, for I always wanted to eat whatever I saw her eating.

Just a few days after this, Miss Laura and I returned to Fairport, and some of Mr. Wood's apples traveled along with us, for he sent a good many to the Boston market. Mr. and Mrs. Wood came to the station to see us off. Mr. Harry could not come, for he had left Riverdale the day before to go back to his college. Mrs. Wood said that she would be very lonely without her two young people, and she kissed Miss Laura over and over again, and made her promise to come back again the next summer.

I was put in a box in the express car, and Mr. Wood told the agent that if he knew what was good for him he would speak to me occasionally, for I was a very knowing dog, and if he didn't treat me well, I'd be apt to write him up in the newspapers. The agent laughed, and quite often on the way to Fairport he came to my box and spoke kindly to me. So I did not get so lonely and frightened as I did on my way to Riverdale.

How glad the Morrises were to see us coming back! The boys had all come home before us, and such a fuss as they did make over their sister! They loved her dearly, and never wanted her to be long away from them. I was rubbed and stroked, and had to run about offering my paw to everyone. Jim and little Billy licked my face, and Bella croaked out, "Glad to see you, Joe. Had a good time? How's your health?"

We soon settled down for the winter. Miss Laura began going to school, and came home every day with a pile of books under her arm. The summer in the country had done her so much good that her mother often looked at her fondly, and said the white-faced child she sent away had come home a nut-brown maid.

33

Performing Animals

Aweek or two after we got home, I heard the Morris boys talking about an Italian who was coming to Fairport with a troupe of trained animals. I could see for myself, whenever I went to town, great flaming pictures on the fences, of monkeys sitting at tables, and of dogs, ponies, and goats climbing ladders and rolling balls and doing various other tricks.

I wondered very much whether they would be able to do all those extraordinary things, but it turned out that they did.

The Italian's name was Bellini, and one afternoon the whole Morris family went to see him and his animals, and when they came home, all they could talk about was the Bellini show.

"I wish you could have been there, Joe," said Jack, pulling

up my paws to rest on his knees. "Now listen, old fellow, and I'll tell you all about it. First of all, there was a perfect jam in the town hall. I sat up in front with a lot of fellows, and had a splendid view.

"The old Italian came out dressed in his best suit of clothes —black broadcloth, flower in his buttonhole, and so on. He made a fine bow, and he said he was 'pleased to see ze fine audience, and I am going to show zem ze fine animals, ze finest in ze world.' Then he shook a little whip that he carried in his hand, and he said, 'Zat whip doesn't mean zat I am cruel.' He cracked it to show his animals when to begin, end, or change their tricks. Some boy yelled, 'Rats! You do whip them sometimes!' And the old man made another bow to his audience and said, 'Sairteenly, I whip zem just as ze mammas whip ze naughty boys, to make zem keep still when zey was noisy or stubborn.'

"Then everybody laughed at the boy, and the Italian said the performance would begin by a grand procession of all the animals, if some lady would kindly step up to the piano and play a march. Nina Smith—you know Nina, Joe, the girl that has black eyes and wears blue ribbons, and lives around the corner—stepped up to the piano and banged out a fine loud march. The doors at the side of the platform opened, and out came the animals, two by two, just like Noah's ark. There was a pony with a monkey walking beside it and holding on to its mane, another monkey on a pony's back, two monkeys hand in hand, a dog with a parrot on his back, a goat harnessed to a little carriage, another goat carrying a bird cage in its mouth with two canaries inside, different kinds of cats, some doves and pigeons, half a dozen white rats with red harness, dragging a little chariot with a monkey in it, and a common white

gander that came in last of all and did nothing but follow one
of the ponies about.

"The Italian spoke of the gander, and said it was a stupid
creature and could do no tricks, and he only kept it on account
of its affection for the pony. He had got them both on a Vermont farm, when he was looking for show animals. The
pony's master had made a pet of him, and had taught him to
come whenever he whistled for him. Though the pony was
only a scrub creature, he had a gentle disposition, and every
other animal on the farm liked him. The gander, in particular,
had such an admiration for him that he followed him wherever he went, and if he lost him for an instant, he would
mount one of the knolls on the farm and stretch out his neck
looking for him. When he caught sight of him, he gabbled
with delight and, running to him, waddled up and down beside him.

"Every little while the pony put his nose down and seemed
to be having a conversation with the goose. If the farmer
whistled for the pony and he started to run to him, the gander,
knowing he could not keep up, would seize the pony's tail in
his beak and, flapping his wings, would get along as fast as
the pony did. And the pony never kicked him. The Italian saw
that this pony would be a good one to train for the stage, so he
offered the farmer a large price for him, and took him away.

"Oh, Joe, I forgot to say that by this time all the animals
had been sent off the stage except the pony and the gander,
and they stood looking at the Italian while he talked. I never
saw anything as human in dumb animals as that pony's face.
He looked as if he understood every word that his master was
saying. After this story was over, the Italian made another
bow, and then told the pony to bow. He nodded his head at

the people, and they all laughed. Then the Italian asked him to favor us with a waltz, and the pony got up on his hind legs and danced.

"You should have seen that gander skirmishing around, so as to be near the pony and yet keep out of the way of his heels. We fellows just roared, and we would have kept him dancing all the afternoon if the Italian hadn't begged 'ze young gentlemen not to make ze noise, but let ze pony do his tricks.'

"Pony number two came on the stage, and it was too queer for anything to see the things the two of them did. They helped the Italian on with his coat, they pulled off his rubbers, they took his coat away and brought him a chair and dragged a table up to it. They brought him letters and papers, and rang bells, and rolled barrels, and swung the Italian in a big swing, and jumped a rope, and walked up and down steps. They just went around that stage as handy with their teeth as two boys would be with their hands, and they seemed to understand every word their master said to them.

"The best trick of all was telling the time and doing questions in arithmetic. The Italian pulled his watch out of his pocket and showed it to the first pony, whose name was Diamond, and said, 'What time is it?' The pony looked at it, then scratched four times with his forefeet on the platform. The Italian said, 'Zat's good—four o'clock. But it's a few minutes after four—how many?' The pony scratched again five times. The Italian showed his watch to the audience, and said that it was just five minutes past four.

"Then he asked the pony how old he was. He scratched four times. That meant four years. He asked him how many days there were in a week and how many months in a year. Then he asked some questions in addition and subtraction, and the pony answered them all correctly. Of course, the Italian was giving him some sign; but, though we watched him closely, we couldn't make out what it was. At last, he told the pony that he had been very good, and had done his lessons well; if it would rest him, he might be naughty a little while.

"All of a sudden a wicked look came into the creature's eyes. He turned around and kicked up his heels at his master; he pushed over the table and chairs, and knocked down a blackboard where he had been rubbing out figures with a sponge held in his mouth. The Italian pretended to be cross, and said, 'Come, come! This won't do!' And he called the other pony to him and told him to take that troublesome fellow off the stage. The second one nosed Diamond and pushed him about, finally bit him by the ear and led him squealing off the stage. The gander followed, gabbling as fast as he could, in a roar of applause.

"After that, there were ladders brought in, Joe, and dogs came on; not thoroughbreds, but curs something like you. The Italian says he can't teach tricks to pedigreed animals as well as to scrubs. Those dogs jumped the ladders, and climbed them, and went through them, and did all kinds of things. The man cracked his whip once, and they began; twice, and they did backward what they had done forward; three times, and they stopped; and all the animals, dogs, goats, ponies, and monkeys, after they had finished their tricks, ran up to their master, and he gave them lumps of sugar. They seemed fond of him, and often when they weren't performing went up to him and licked his hands or his sleeve.

"There was one boss dog, Joe, with a head like yours. Bob, they called him, and he did all of his tricks alone. The Italian went off the stage, and the dog came on and made his bow, and climbed his ladders, and jumped his hurdles, and went off again. The audience howled for an encore, and didn't he come out alone, make another bow, and retire! I saw old Judge Brown wiping the tears from his eyes, he'd laughed so much. One of the last tricks was with a goat, and the Italian said it was the best of all, because the goat is such a hard animal to teach. He had a big ball, and the goat got on it and rolled it across the stage without getting off. He looked as nervous as a cat, shaking his old beard and trying to keep his four hoofs close enough together to keep him on the ball.

"We had a funny little play at the end of the performance. A monkey, dressed as a lady in a white satin suit and a bonnet with a white veil, came on the stage. She was Miss Green and the dog Bob was going to elope with her. He was all rigged out as Mr. Smith, and had on a light suit of clothes, with a high collar and long cuffs, and a tall hat on the side of his head, and he carried a cane. He was a regular dude. He stepped up to Miss Green on his hind legs, and helped her onto a pony's back. Then the pony galloped off the stage.

"Then a crowd of monkeys, chattering and wringing their hands, came on. Mr. Smith had run away with their child! They were all dressed up, too. There were the father and mother, with gray wigs and black clothes, and the young Greens in bibs and tuckers. They were a queer-looking crowd. While they were going on in this way, the pony trotted back on the stage. They all flew at him and pulled off their daughter from his back, and laughed and chattered, and boxed her ears, and took off her white veil and her satin dress, and put on an old brown thing, and some of them seized the dog, and kicked his hat, and broke his cane, and stripped his clothes off, and threw them into a corner, and bound his legs with cords.

"A goat came on, harnessed to a little cart, and they threw the dog in it and wheeled him around the stage a few times. Then they took him out and tied him to a hook in the wall, and the goat ran off the stage, and the monkeys ran to one side, and one of them pulled out a little revolver, pointed it at the dog, fired, and he dropped down as if dead. Everybody in the room clapped and shouted, and then the curtain dropped, and the thing was over."

Jack pushed my paws from his knees and went outdoors, and I began to think that I would very much like to see these performing animals. It was not yet teatime, and I would have plenty of time to take a run down to the hotel where they were staying. So I set out. It was a lovely autumn evening. The sun was going down in a haze, and it was quite warm. Earlier in the day I had heard Mr. Morris say that this was our Indian summer, and that we should soon have cold weather.

Fairport was a pretty little town, and from the principal street one could look out upon the blue water of the bay and see the island opposite, which was quite deserted now, for the summer visitors had gone home.

The Fairport hotel was built right in the center of the town, and the shops and houses crowded quite close about it. It was a high brick building, and it was called the Fairport House. As I was running along the sidewalk I heard someone speak to me, and looking up I saw Charlie Montague. I had heard the Morrises say that his parents were staying at the hotel for a few weeks, while their house was being repaired. He had his Irish setter Brisk with him, and a handsome dog he was, as he stood waving his silky tail in the sunlight. Charlie patted me, and then he and his dog went into the hotel.

I turned into the stable yard. The hotel horses were just

getting rubbed down after their day's work, and others were
coming in. There were no signs of strange animals around the
horses' stable.

I went around to the back of the yard. Here they were, in
an empty cow stable under a hay loft. There were two little
ponies tied up in a stall, two goats beyond them, and dogs and
monkeys in strong traveling cages. I stood in the doorway and
stared at them. I was sorry for the dogs to be shut up on such
a lovely evening, but I suppose their master was afraid of
their getting lost, or being stolen, if he let them loose.

They all seemed very friendly. The ponies turned around
and looked at me with their gentle eyes, and then went on
munching their hay. I wondered very much where the gander
was, and went a little farther into the stable. Something white
raised itself up on the brownest pony's crib, and there was the
gander close up beside the mouth of his friend. The monkeys
made a jabbering sound; the dogs sniffed the air.

While I was peering through the bars at the animals, a man
came in the stable. He noticed me the first thing, but instead
of driving me out, he spoke kindly to me, in a language that
I did not understand. So I knew that he was the Italian. How
glad the animals were to see him! He laughed and talked back
to them. He had a bag on his arm, and he took out bones for
the dogs, nuts and cakes for the monkeys, carrots for the
ponies, some green stuff for the goats, and corn for the gander. It was a pretty sight to see the old man feeding his pets,
and it made me feel quite hungry. So I trotted home.

I was sleeping soundly in my kennel that night with Jim,
when I started up and ran outside. There was a distant bell
ringing, which we often heard in Fairport, and which always
meant fire.

34

A Fire in Fairport

Jim and I ran around to the front of the house. In a few minutes Mr. Morris came rattling to the front door, as we knew he would. Without a word to us, he set off toward the town. We followed after him, and as we hurried along, other men ran out from the houses along the streets, and either joined him or dashed ahead to see what had happened.

"Where's the fire?" they shouted to each other. "Don't know—afraid it's the hotel or the town hall, it's such a blaze. Hope not. How's the water supply? Bad time to have a fire."

It was the hotel. We saw that as soon as we got to the main street. When we got nearer the burning building, we saw men carrying ladders and axes, and heard others shouting directions. Some were rushing out of the hotel with boxes and bundles and furniture in their arms. From the windows above came a steady stream of articles, thrown among the crowd. A mirror struck Mr. Morris on the arm, and a whole package of clothes fell on his head. There was something the matter with Mr. Morris—I knew by the worried sound of his voice when he spoke to anyone. I could not see his face, though it was as light as day about us, for we had got jammed in the crowd, and if I had not kept between his feet, I should have been trodden to death. Jim, being larger than I was, had got separated from us.

Presently Mr. Morris raised his voice above the uproar, and called, "Is everyone out of the hotel?" A voice shouted back, "I'm going up to see."

"It's Jim Watson, the fireman," cried someone near. "He's risking his life to go into that pit of flame."

"Where are the Montagues?" shouted Mr. Morris. "Has anyone seen the Montagues?"

"Mr. Morris! Mr. Morris!" said a frightened voice, and young Charlie Montague pressed through the people to us. "Where's Papa?"

"I don't know. Where did you leave him?" said Mr. Morris, taking his hand and drawing him closer to him. "I was sleeping in his room," said the boy, "and a man knocked at the door and said, 'Hotel on fire. Five minutes to dress and get out.' Papa told me to put on my clothes and go downstairs, and he ran up to Mamma."

"Where was she?" asked Mr. Morris quickly.

"On the fourth floor. She and her maid Blanche were up there. You know, Mamma hasn't been well and couldn't sleep, and our room was so noisy that she moved upstairs where it was quiet." Mr. Morris gave a kind of groan. "Oh, I'm so hot, and there's such a dreadful noise," said the little boy, bursting into tears, "and I want Mamma." Mr. Morris soothed him as best he could, and drew him a little to the edge of the crowd.

While he was doing this, there was a piercing cry. I could not see the person making it, but I knew it was the Italian's voice. He was screaming in broken English that the fire was spreading to the stables and his animals would be burned. Would no one help him to get his animals out? There was a great deal of confused language. Some voices shouted, "Look after the people first. Let the animals go." And others said, "For shame. Get the horses out." But no one seemed to do anything, for the Italian went on crying for help. I heard a number of people who were standing near us say that it had just been found out that several persons who had been sleeping in the top of the hotel had not got out. They said that at one of the top windows a poor housemaid was shrieking for help. Here in the street we could see no one at the upper windows, for smoke was pouring from them.

The air was very hot and heavy, and I didn't wonder that Charlie Montague felt ill. Charlie lay in Mr. Morris's arms and moaned. Mr. Morris was terribly uneasy. He turned his eyes from the great sheets of flame and strained the little boy to his breast.

At last there were wild shrieks that I knew came from no human throats. The fire must have reached the horses. Mr. Morris sprang up, then sank back again. He wanted to go, yet he could be of no use. There were hundreds of men standing about, but the fire had spread so rapidly, and they had so little water to put on it, that there was very little they could do. I wondered whether I could do anything for the poor animals. There was a narrow lane running up a short distance toward the hotel, and I started to go up this, when in front of me I heard such a wailing, piercing noise that it made me shudder and stand still. The Italian's animals were going to be burned up, and they were calling to their master to come and let them out. I could not stand it.

Then I stumbled over something. It was a large bird—a parrot—and at first I thought it was Bella. Then I remembered hearing Jack say that the Italian had a parrot. It was not dead, but seemed stupid from the smoke. I seized it in my mouth, and ran and laid it at Mr. Morris's feet. He wrapped it in his handkerchief, and laid it beside him.

I shall never forget that dreadful night. It seemed as if we were there for hours, but in reality it was only a short time. The hotel soon got to be all red flames, and there was little smoke. The inside of the building had been burned away, and nothing more could be taken out. A man stepped quietly up to Mr. Morris and, looking at him, I saw that it was Mr. Montague. He was usually a well-dressed man, with a kind face and a head of thick, grayish-brown hair. Now his face was black and grimy, his hair was burned from the front of his head, and his clothes were half torn from his back. Mr. Morris sprang up when he saw him, and said, "Where is your wife?"

The gentleman did not say a word, but pointed to the burning building. "Impossible!" cried Mr. Morris. "Is there no mistake? Your beautiful young wife, Montague. Can it really be so?" Mr. Morris was trembling from head to foot.

"It is true," said Mr. Montague quietly, and though I am only a dog, I knew his heart was breaking. "Give me the boy."

In the morning the boys went downtown before breakfast and learned all about the fire. It started in the top story of the hotel, in the room of some foolish young men who were sitting up late playing cards. One of them upset a lamp, and when the flames began to spread so that they could not extinguish them, instead of rousing someone near them, they had rushed downstairs to get someone there to come up and help them put out the fire. When they returned with some of the hotel people, they found that the flames had spread from their room, which was in an "L" at the back of the house, to the front part, where Mrs. Montague's room was, and where the housemaids belonging to the hotel slept. By this time Mr. Montague had rushed upstairs. But he found the passageway to his wife's room so full of flames and smoke that though he tried again and again to force his way through, he could not. He disappeared for a time. Then he came to Mr. Morris, with whom he had left Charlie, and got his boy and took him to some rooms over his bank and shut himself up. For some days he would let no one in. Then he came out with the look of an old man on his face, and his hair as white as snow, and went out to his beautiful house in the outskirts of town.

The Morris boys said that they found the old Italian sitting on an empty box, looking at the smoking ruins of the hotel. His head was hanging on his breast, and his eyes were full of tears. His ponies were burned up, he said, and the gander, and the monkeys, and the goats, and his wonderful performing dogs. He had his birds left, he said, all except his parrot, and that was all. He was a ruined man.

Jack told him that they had the parrot safe at home, and that it was very much alive, and quarreling furiously with Bella. The old man's face brightened at this, and then Jack and Carl, finding that he had had no breakfast, went off to a restaurant nearby and got him some steak and coffee.

At teatime Mr. Morris went downtown to see that the Italian got a comfortable place for the night. When he came back, he said that he had found out that the Italian was by no means so old a man as he looked, and that he had talked to him about raising a sum of money for him among the Fairport people, till he had become quite cheerful, and said that if Mr. Morris would do that, he would try to gather another troupe of animals together and train them to perform.

"Now, what can we do for this Italian?" asked Mrs. Morris. "We can't give him much money, but we might let him have one or two of our pets. There's Billy. He's a bright little dog, and not two years old yet. The Italian could teach him anything."

There was a blank silence among the Morris children. Billy was such a gentle, lovable little dog that he was a favorite with everyone in the house.

There was a good deal of discussion, but the end of it was that Billy was given to the Italian. He came up to get him and was very grateful and made a great many bows, holding his hat in his hand. Billy took to him at once, and the Italian spoke so kindly to him that we knew he would have a good master. Mr. Morris got quite a large sum of money for him, and when he handed it to him, the poor man was so pleased that he kissed his hand and promised to send frequent word of Billy's progress and welfare.

35

Dandy the Tramp

ABOUT A week after Billy left us, the Morris family, much to its surprise, became the owner of a new dog.

He walked into the house one cold wintry afternoon and lay calmly down by the fire. He was a brindled bull terrier, and he had on a silver-plated collar with "Dandy" engraved on it. He lay all the evening by the fire, and when any of the family spoke to him, he wagged his tail and looked pleased. I growled a little at him at first, but he never cared a bit and just dozed off to sleep, and so I soon stopped.

He was such a well-bred dog that the Morrises were afraid that someone had lost him. They made some inquiries the next day and found that he belonged to a New York gentleman who had come to Fairport in the summer in a yacht. Dandy

came ashore in a boat whenever he got a chance, and if he
could not come in a boat, he would swim. He was a tramp,
his master said, and he wouldn't stay long in any place. The
Morrises were so amused with his impudence that they did
not send him away, but said every day, "Surely he will be gone
tomorrow."

However, Mr. Dandy was in comfortable quarters and he
had no intention of changing them, for a while at least. He
was very handsome and had such a pleasant way with him
that the family could not help liking him. I never cared for
him. He fawned on the Morrises and pretended he loved
them, and afterward turned around and laughed and sneered
at them in a way that made me very angry. I used to lecture
him sometimes, and growl about him to Jim, but Jim always
said, "Let him alone. You can't do him any good. He was born
bad. His mother wasn't good. He tells me that she had a bad
name among all the dogs in her neighborhood. She was a thief
and a runaway."

We were lying out in the sun one day on the platform at
the back of the house, and Dandy had been more than usually
provoking; so I got up to leave him. He put himself in my way,
however, and said coaxingly, "Don't be cross, old fellow. I'll
tell you some stories to amuse you, old boy. What shall they be
about?"

"I think the story of your life would be about as interesting
as anything you could make up," I said dryly as I looked at
him.

"All right, fact or fiction, whichever you like. Here's a fact,
plain and unvarnished. Born and bred in New York. Swell
stable. Swell coachman. Swell master. Jeweled fingers of
ladies poking at me, first thing I remember. But," he went on

coolly, "when I was a few months old, I began to find the stable yard narrow, and wondered what there was outside of it. I discovered a hole in the garden wall, and used to sneak out nights. Oh, what fun it was! I got to know a lot of street dogs, and we had gay times, barking under people's windows and making them mad, and getting into back yards and chasing cats. Policemen would chase us, and we would run. Then I'd go home and sleep all day, and go out again the next night.

"When I was about a year old, I began to stay out days as well as nights. They couldn't keep me home. Then I ran away for three months. I got with an old lady on Fifth Avenue, who was very fond of dogs. She had four white poodles, and her servants used to wash them and tie up their hair with blue ribbons, and she used to take them for drives in her phaeton in the park, and they wore gold and silver collars. I went driving, too, and sometimes we met my master. He smiled and shook his head at me. I heard him tell the coachman one day that I was a little blackguard, but he was to let me come and go as I liked."

"If they had whipped you soundly," I said, "it might have made a good dog of you."

"I'm good enough now," said Dandy airily. "The young ladies who drove with my master used to say that it was priggish and tiresome to be too good. I stayed with Mrs. Judge Tibbett till I got sick of her fussy ways. When I left her, I ran away to her niece's, Miss Ball's. She was a sensible young lady, and she used to scold her aunt for the way in which she brought up her dogs. But then Miss Ball was fussy in her way, too. Her pug and I were rubbed and scrubbed within an inch of our lives, and had to go for such long walks that I got thoroughly sick of them.

"A woman whom the servants called Trotsey came every morning, and took the pug and me by our chains, and sometimes another dog or two, and took us for a long tramp in quiet streets. That was Trotsey's business, to walk dogs, and Miss Ball got a great many fashionable young ladies who could not exercise their dogs to let Trotsey have them, and they said it made a great difference in the health and appearance of their pets. Trotsey got fifteen cents an hour for a dog. Goodness, what appetites those walks gave us, and didn't we make the dog biscuits disappear afterward!

"But it was a slow life at Miss Ball's. We only saw her for a little while every day. She slept till noon. After lunch she played with us for a little while in the greenhouse, and then she was off driving or visiting, and in the evening she always had company or went to a dance or to the theatre. I soon made up my mind that I'd run away. I jumped out of a window one fine morning and ran home. I stayed there for a long time. My master never bothered his head about me, and I could do as I liked.

"One day I was having a walk and meeting a lot of dogs that I knew. A little boy came behind me, and before I could tell what he was doing, he had snatched me up and was running off with me. I couldn't bite him, for he had stuffed some rags in my mouth. He took me to a tenement house, in a part of the city that I had never been in before. He belonged to a very poor family. My faith, weren't they badly off—six children, and a mother and father, all living in two tiny rooms. Scarcely a bit of meat did I smell while I was there. I hated their bread and molasses.

"They kept me shut up in their dirty rooms for several days, and the brat of a boy that caught me slept with his arm around me at night. The weather was hot and sometimes we couldn't sleep, and they had to go up on the roof. After a while, they chained me up in a filthy yard at the back of the house, and there I thought I should go mad. I would have liked to bite them, if I had dared. I was there a month, while they were waiting for a reward to be offered. But none came. And one day the boy's father, who was a street peddler, took me by my chain and led me about the streets till he sold me. A gentleman got me for his little boy, but I didn't like the look of him. I sprang up and bit his hand, and he dropped the chain, and I dodged boys and policemen, and finally got home more dead than alive and looking like a skeleton. I had a good time for several weeks, and then I began to get restless and was off again. But I'm getting tired. I want to go to sleep."

I sat and looked at him. What a handsome, good-natured, worthless dog he was! A few days later, he told me the rest of his history. After a great many wanderings, he happened home one day just as his master's yacht was going to sail, and they chained him up till they went on board, so that he could be an amusement on the passage to Fairport.

It was in November that Dandy came to us, and he stayed all winter. He made fun of the Morrises all the time, and said they had a dull, poky, old house, and he only stayed because of Miss Laura. But I knew he was just waiting for the first fine day of spring to be off; and he was. During the rest of the spring and summer we met him occasionally running about town with a set of fast dogs. One day I stopped and asked him how he contented himself in such a quiet place as Fairport, and he said he was dying to get back to New York and was hoping that his master's yacht would come and take him away.

Poor Dandy never left Fairport. After all, he was not such

a bad dog. There was nothing really vicious about him, and I hate to speak of his end. His master's yacht did not come, and soon the summer was over, and the winter was coming, and no one wanted Dandy, for he had such a bad name. He got hungry and cold, and one day sprang upon a little girl, to take away a piece of bread and butter she was eating. He did not see the large house dog on the door sill, and before he could get away, the dog had seized him and bitten and shaken him till he was nearly dead. When the dog threw him aside, he crawled to the Morrises, and Miss Laura bandaged his wounds and made him a bed in the stable.

One Sunday morning she washed and fed him tenderly, for she knew he could not live much longer. He was so weak that he could scarcely eat the food that she put in his mouth. As she was going to church, I could not go with her, but I ran down the lane and watched her out of sight. When I came back Dandy was gone. I looked till I found him. He had crawled into the darkest corner of the stable to die. Poor Dandy! Poor, handsome dog of a rich master, who hadn't thought it important to raise him properly. A young pup should be trained just as a child is, and punished when he goes wrong. Dandy began badly, and not being checked in his evil ways, had come to this.

When Miss Laura came home, she cried bitterly to know that he was dead. The boys took him away from her, and made him a grave in the corner of the garden.

36

The End of My Story

I HAVE come now to the last chapter of my story. I thought when I began to write, that I would put down the events of each year of my life, but I fear that would make my story too long, and neither Miss Laura nor any boys and girls would care to read it. So I will just stop here, though I would gladly go on, for I have enjoyed so much talking over old times that I am very sorry to leave off now.

Every year that I have been at the Morrises' something pleasant has happened to me, but I cannot put all these things down, nor can I tell how Miss Laura and the boys grew and changed, year by year, till now they are quite grown-up. I will just bring my tale down to the present time; then I will stop talking, and go lie down in my basket, for I am an old dog now and get tired very easily.

I was a year old when I went to the Morrises, and I have been with them for twelve years. I am not living in the same house with Mr. and Mrs. Morris now, but I am with my dear Miss Laura, who is Miss Laura no longer, but Mrs. Gray. She married Mr. Harry four years ago, and lives with him and Mr. and Mrs. Wood on Dingley Farm. Mr. and Mrs. Morris live in a cottage nearby. Mr. Morris is not very strong and can preach no longer. The boys are all scattered. Jack married pretty Miss Bessie Drury, and lives on a large farm near here. Carl is a merchant in New York, Ned is a clerk in a bank, and Willie is studying at a place called Harvard.

The Morrises' old friends often come to see them. Mrs. Drury comes every summer on her way to Newport, and Mr. Montague and Charlie come every other summer. Charlie always brings with him his old dog Brisk, who is getting feeble, like myself. We lie on the veranda in the sunshine, and sometimes it makes us feel quite young again. In addition to Brisk we have a Scotch collie. He is very handsome and is a constant attendant of Miss Laura's. We are great friends, he and I, but he can get about much better than I can. One day a friend of Miss Laura's came with a little boy and girl, and Collie sat between the two children, and their father took their picture with a Kodak. I like him so much that I told him I would try to get them to put his picture in my book.

When the Morris boys are all here in the summer, we have gay times. All through the winter we look forward to their coming, for they make the old farmhouse so lively. Mr. Maxwell never misses a summer in coming to Riverdale. He has such a following of dumb animals now that he says he can't move them any farther away from Boston than this, and he doesn't know what he will do with them unless he sets up a menagerie. He asked Miss Laura the other day if she thought the old Italian would take him into partnership. He did not know what had happened to poor Bellini, and so Miss Laura told him.

A few years ago the Italian came to Riverdale to exhibit his new stock of performing animals. They were almost as good as the old ones, but he had not quite so many as he had before. The Morrises and a great many of their friends went to his performance, and Miss Laura said afterward that when cunning little Billy came on the stage, made his bow, and went through his antics of jumping through hoops and catching balls, she almost had hysterics.

The Italian had made a special pet of him for the Morrises' sake, and treated him more like a human being than a dog. Billy rather put on airs when he came up to the farm to see us, but he was such a dear little dog, in spite of being almost spoiled by his master, that Jim and I could not get angry with him. In a few days they went away, and we heard nothing but good news from them, till last winter. Then a letter came to Miss Laura from a nurse in a New York hospital. She said that the Italian was very near his end, and he wanted her to write to Mrs. Gray to tell her that he had sold all his animals but the little dog that she had so kindly given him. He was sending him back to her, and with his last breath he would pray for heaven's blessing on the kind lady and her family that had befriended him when he was in trouble.

The next day Billy arrived, a thin white scarecrow of a dog. He was sick and unhappy and would eat nothing, and started up at the slightest sound. He was listening for the Italian's footsteps, but Bellini never came, and one day Mr. Harry looked up from his newspaper and said, "Laura, Bellini is dead." Miss Laura's eyes filled with tears, and Billy, who had jumped up when he heard his master's name, fell back again. He knew what they meant, and from that instant he ceased listening for footsteps, and lay quite still till he died. Miss Laura had him put in a little wooden box and buried him in a corner of the garden, and when she is working among her flowers, she often speaks regretfully of him, and of poor Dandy, who lies in the garden at Fairport.

Bella, the parrot, lives with Mrs. Morris and is as smart as ever. I have heard that parrots live to a very great age. Some of them even get to be a hundred years old. If that is the case, Bella will outlive all of us. She notices that I am getting blind and feeble, and when I go down to call on Mrs. Morris, she calls out to me, "Keep a stiff upper lip, Beautiful Joe. Never say die, Beautiful Joe. Keep the game a-going, Beautiful Joe."

Mrs. Morris says that she doesn't know where Bella picks up her slang words. I think it is Mr. Ned who teaches her, for when he comes home in the summer, he often says, with a sly twinkle in his eye, "Come out into the garden, Bella." And he lies in a hammock under the trees, and Bella perches on a branch near him, and he talks to her by the hour. Anyway, it is in autumn after he leaves that Bella always shocks Mrs. Morris with her slang talk.

I am glad I am living in Riverdale. Fairport was a very nice place, but it was not open and free like this farm. I take a walk every morning that the sun shines. I go out among the horses and cows and stop to watch the hens pecking at their food. This is a happy place, and I hope my dear Miss Laura will live to enjoy it many years after I am gone.

I have very few worries. The pigs bother me a little in the

spring by rooting up the bones that I bury in the fields in the fall, but that is a small matter, and I try not to mind it. I get a great many bones here, and I should be glad if I had some poor city dogs to help me eat them. I don't think bones are good for pigs.

Then there is Mr. Harry's tame squirrel out in one of the barns that teases me considerably. He knows that I can't chase him, now that my legs are so stiff with rheumatism, and he takes delight in showing me how spry he can be, darting around me and whisking his tail almost in my face, and trying to get me to run after him, so that he can laugh at me. I don't think that he is a very thoughtful squirrel, but I try not to notice him.

The sailor boy who gave Bella to the Morrises has got to be a large, stout man, and is the first mate of a vessel. He sometimes comes here, and when he does, he always brings the Morrises presents of foreign fruits and curiosities of different kinds.

Malta, the cat, is still living with Mrs. Morris. Davy, the rat, is gone, and so is poor old Jim. He went away one day last summer, and no one ever knew what became of him. The Morrises searched everywhere for him, and offered a large reward to anyone who would find him, but he never turned up again. I think that he felt he was going to die, and went into some out-of-the-way place. He remembered how badly Miss Laura felt when Dandy died, and he wanted to spare her the greater sorrow of his death. He was always such a thoughtful dog, and so anxious not to give trouble. I am more selfish. I could not go away from Miss Laura, even to die. When my last hour comes, I want to see her gentle face bending over me, and then I shall not mind how much I suffer.

She is just as tenderhearted as ever, but she tries not to feel too bad about the sorrow and suffering in the world, because she says that would weaken her, and she wants all her strength to try to put a stop to some of it. She does a great deal of good in Riverdale, and I do not think there is anyone in all the country around who is as much beloved as she is.

She has never forgotten the resolve that she made some years ago, that she would do all she could to protect dumb creatures. Mr. Harry and Mr. Maxwell have helped her nobly. Mr. Maxwell's work is largely done in Boston, and Miss Laura and Mr. Harry have to do most of theirs by writing, for Riverdale has got to be a model village with respect to the treatment of all kinds of animals. It is a model village not only in that respect, but in others. It has seemed as if all other improvements went hand in hand with the humane treatment of animals. Thoughtfulness toward lower creatures has made the people more and more thoughtful toward themselves, and this little town is getting to have quite a name through the state for its good schools, good society, and good business and religious standing. Many people are moving into it to educate their children. The Riverdale people are very particular about what sort of strangers come to live among them.

A man who came here two years ago and opened a shop was seen kicking a small kitten out of his house. The next day a committee of Riverdale citizens waited on him and said they had had a great deal of trouble to root out cruelty from the village, and they didn't want anyone to come there and introduce it again, and they thought he had better move on to some other place.

The man was utterly astonished, and said he'd never heard of such particular people. He had had no thought of being cruel. He didn't think that the kitten cared. But now when he turned the thing over in his mind, he didn't suppose cats liked being kicked about any more than he would like it himself, and he would promise to be kind to them in future. He said, too, that if they had no objection, he would just stay on, for if the people there treated dumb animals with such consideration, they would certainly treat human beings better, and he thought it would be a good place to bring up his children. Of course they let him stay, and he is now a man who is celebrated for his kindness to every living thing. And he never refuses to help Miss Laura when she goes to him for money to carry out any of her humane schemes.

Before I close, I must put in one important saying of Miss Laura's that comes out of her years of service for dumb animals. She says that cruel and vicious owners of animals should be punished, but to merely thoughtless people, don't say "Don't" so much. Don't go to them and say, "Don't overfeed your animals, and don't starve them, and don't overwork them, and don't beat them," and so on through a long list of hardships that can be put upon suffering animals.

Simply say, "Be kind. Make a study of your animal's wants, and see that they are satisfied. No one can tell you how to treat your animal as well as you should know yourself, for you are with it all the time, and know its disposition, and just how much work it can stand, and how much rest and food it needs, and just how it is different from every other animal. If it is sick and unhappy, you are the one to take care of it, for nearly every animal loves its own master better than a stranger and will get well quicker under his care."

Miss Laura says that if men and women are kind in every respect to their dumb servants, they will be astonished to find how much happiness they will bring into their lives, and how faithful and grateful their dumb animals will be to them.

Now I must really close my story. Good-bye to the boys and girls who may read it; and if it is not wrong for a dog to say it, I should like to add, "God bless you all." If in my feeble way I have been able to impress you with the fact that dogs and many other animals love their masters and mistresses, and live only to please them, my little story will not be written in vain. My last words are, "Boys and girls, be kind to dumb animals, not only because you will lose nothing by it, but because you ought to; for they were placed on the earth by the same kind Hand that made all living creatures."